**What was Indiana Jones doing
in Athens in January 1914?**

Indiana Jones is that world-famous, whip-cracking hero you know from the movies...

But was he *always* cool and fearless in the face of danger? Did he *always* get mixed up in hair-raising, heart-stopping escapades?

Yes!

Read all about Indy as a kid. Watch him plunge into deep water when he goes after an antique gold bowl and the mysterious museum thief who stole it. Get ready for some edge-of-your-seat excitement!

YOUNG INDIANA JONES BOOKS
(original novels)

Young Indiana Jones and the...
1. Plantation Treasure
2. Tomb of Terror
3. Circle of Death
4. Secret City
5. Princess of Peril
6. Gypsy Revenge
7. Ghostly Riders
8. Curse of the Ruby Cross
9. Titanic Adventure
10. Lost Gold of Durango
11. Face of the Dragon
12. Journey to the Underworld
13. Mountain of Fire
14. Pirates' Loot
15. Eye of the Tiger

THE YOUNG INDIANA JONES CHRONICLES
(novels based on the television series)

TV-1. The Mummy's Curse
TV-2. Field of Death
TV-3. Safari Sleuth
TV-4. The Secret Peace
TV-5. Trek of Doom
TV-6. Revolution!
TV-7. Race to Danger
TV-8. Prisoner of War

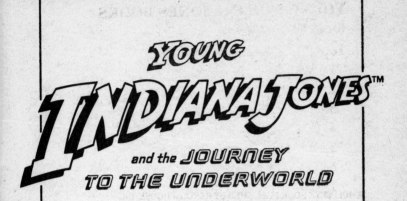

YOUNG INDIANA JONES™
and the JOURNEY
TO THE UNDERWORLD

By Megan Stine &
H. William Stine

Bullseye Books

Random House New York

A BULLSEYE BOOK PUBLISHED BY RANDOM HOUSE, INC.

Copyright © 1994 by Lucasfilm Ltd. (LFL)
Young Indy novels are conceived and produced by Random House, Inc.,
in conjunction with Lucasfilm Ltd.

Library of Congress Cataloging-in-Publication Data:
Stine, Megan.
Young Indiana Jones and the journey to the underworld / by Megan
Stine and H. William Stine.
    p. cm. — (Young Indiana Jones books ; #12)
"Bullseye books."
SUMMARY: While seaching for a stolen golden bowl in Athens, young
Indiana Jones finds himself reliving the legend of the ancient Greek
hero Orpheus.
ISBN 0-679-85458-4
1. Orpheus (Greek mythology)—Juvenile fiction. [1. Orpheus
(Greek mythology)—Fiction. 2. Adventure and adventurers—Fiction.]
I. Stine, H. William. II. Title. III. Series.
PZ7.S86035Yn   1994   [Fic]—dc20   93-36821

Manufactured in the United States of America 10 9 8 7 6 5 4 3 2

Chapter 1

"Don't touch that!" barked a voice that echoed through the whole museum gallery.

Young Indiana Jones froze. A huge hand clamped down hard on his shoulder, startling him. Indy jumped so much, he nearly dropped the precious golden bowl he was holding.

"Put it back, mate!" ordered the tall, burly museum guard, who was still gripping Indy's shoulder.

"It's all right, Johnson," called a well-dressed gentleman who moved quickly across the marble floor. Indy recognized Eric Scythe, one of the curators of the British Museum in London.

"Whatever you say, Mr. Scythe," the guard said, backing off.

As soon as Indy felt the grip on his shoulder relax, he carefully set the golden bowl back on its pedestal.

"This is young Henry Jones, the son of an old college friend of mine," Eric Scythe explained to the guard. "I've given him permission to handle whatever he likes in the museum."

"I see, sir," the guard said.

"What's happened?" Indy's father called. "Is everything all right?"

Professor Henry Jones hurried toward them, stuffing a notebook into the pocket of his tweed jacket. His brown beard and hair matched the color of the patches on his sleeves.

"Everything's fine, Henry," Eric Scythe said in his crisp British accent. "Do calm down. Johnson is worrying enough for everyone."

As the guard walked away, Indy immediately picked up the golden bowl again. It was light and delicate. Inside were drawings of Greek gods and goddesses etched in the metal.

"Look, Dad," Indy said.

"Ah, the Pietroasa bowl. I've been wanting to see it myself," said Professor Jones.

"Hold it carefully, Junior. I understand it's over sixteen hundred years old."

Dad, Indy thought, I'm fourteen! I know the difference between a priceless bowl and a football!

But before Indy could say anything, a loud voice from the other side of the room caught everyone's attention.

"'Ere, slow down, Master Reggie!" cried a large woman. "Wait for yer old nanny!"

Indy turned to watch a little boy in a sailor suit sprinting across the wide marble floor. His long blond curls bounced as he ran. He was being chased by a woman whose gray hair was quickly escaping from under a small black hat. From her manner, Indy knew she was a typical British nanny, a sort of live-in babysitter.

"Master Reggie, wait!" she called again.

The boy laughed as he darted in and out among the statues and other treasures that rested on marble pedestals.

"Catch me, Nanny. Catch me!" the boy called over his shoulder when he was a few feet from Indy.

"Hey! Watch out!" Indy yelled.

But it was too late. Reggie ran full force

into Indy, knocking him sideways. With an "oomph!" Indy stumbled into the marble pedestal. His wide-brimmed brown felt hat flew off as he fell toward the floor. At the same time, the pedestal began to topple— and the bowl flew out of Indy's hands.

"The Pietroasa bowl!" cried Professor Jones.

Everything that happened next was a blur. All Indy heard was a jumble of sounds. His father and Eric Scythe gasping in horror. Reggie hollering as he tumbled to the floor. The clank of the bowl hitting the polished marble surface. And worst of all— the heavy marble pedestal crashing down, crushing the golden bowl flat.

As soon as the nanny reached them, she pulled Reggie to his feet. "Now say yer sorry to the boy, Master Reggie," she demanded.

The boy smiled devilishly up into her face and didn't say a word.

"Say you're *sorry*?" Professor Jones sputtered. "Madam, do you have *any* idea what he's done?"

The woman looked coldly at Professor Jones. "'E ran into your son," she said. "I got eyes, you know."

In shock, Indy got to his feet. His light brown hair was in his eyes, and his face felt hot and red. How could this have happened while *he* was holding the Pietroasa bowl?

Shaking, Indy helped Eric Scythe move the pedestal. But even before he picked up the bowl, Indy could see that it wasn't a bowl anymore. Now it looked like a golden pancake.

"He's destroyed a priceless antiquity!" Professor Jones said to the woman.

"Well, I'm sure 'e didn't mean to," said the nanny. "'E's just a litt-ul boy, you know. Accidents will 'appen."

She turned quickly and walked away, pulling Reggie along behind her.

Indy saw the agonized expression on his father's face and felt even worse.

"I'm really sorry, Mr. Scythe," Indy said, swallowing hard. "It's my fault. I should have held on to it tighter."

Eric Scythe's face was colorless. But somehow he forced himself to keep speaking in his quiet, civilized voice. "Do come to my office, if you would, Henry," he said. "There's something we must discuss."

Without a word, Indy followed Eric

Scythe and his father to a small office in the back of the British Museum. There a large fire snapped and jumped in a stone fireplace. Scythe sat down behind a large desk with a green leather top. He gestured for Indy and his father to sit in the two leather chairs facing him.

"I feel terrible about this, Eric," said Professor Jones. Indy noticed that his father was perspiring. "Absolutely terrible."

Scythe was quiet for a moment. He seemed to be collecting his thoughts. At last he said, "There's no need to feel quite so badly." He reached across the desk and handed the smashed bowl to Indy's father. "You see, Henry, it's a replica."

Professor Jones almost dropped the flattened object. "A copy? By Jove, Eric!" he exclaimed. "You mean we *didn't* smash the Pietroasa bowl?"

"That's right, old man. The museum made an exact copy when the real bowl was on loan here in the mid-1800s."

Indy's father took a long, relieved breath. Finally Indy felt safe to take one too. "Then you can make another replica," he said.

"We could," said Scythe. "We could, that

10

is, if the real bowl hadn't been stolen."

"Good heavens!" said Professor Jones.

The museum curator leaned back in his chair. "I've already told you more than I should have," he said. "But I can't bear the weight of this secret alone any longer. Especially not now," he added, glancing at the flattened bowl.

"Eric, what is it?" Professor Jones asked.

Scythe unlocked a desk drawer with a small brass key and removed an envelope. "This is in strict confidence, old friend," said Scythe.

"Of course," said Professor Jones.

"Me too," said Indy.

Scythe nodded and opened the envelope. "This letter is from a friend of mine in Rumania. That is where the original Pietroasa bowl was found, so naturally that's where it belongs," he said. "The letter is dated two weeks ago, January 3, 1914, and it is, as you Yanks say, short and sweet. It says simply that the bowl was stolen from a public display in broad daylight, although no one actually saw who stole it."

Eric Scythe looked up from the letter. "Please understand: this is a great embarrassment for my Rumanian friend. He has written only to me and to one other man about the theft—and now I have told you. That makes just five of us who know. And it must remain that way."

"You're forgetting someone," said Indy. "The thief."

"You mean, Markos Kourou?" asked Mr. Scythe.

Indy gaped in confusion. "You know who the thief is?"

"Quite so," Scythe answered. "He is a notorious thief of ancient art treasures who lives in Greece."

"Then for heaven's sake, Eric, why don't you have the man arrested?" asked Professor Jones.

"Arrest Kourou?" Scythe asked, as if it had never occurred to him.

"That's what we'd do with him in America," Indy said with a wry smile.

"Ah, but tell me, lad," said Scythe, "how do you arrest a man no one has ever seen?"

"I don't get it," said Indy. "If no one knows what the guy looks like, how do you know *he* took the bowl?"

"Because someone in the museum saw a

Medusa-head cane," answered Eric Scythe. "And that is Markos Kourou's trademark. The top of his cane has a Medusa head made of pure gold. He is never without it."

Medusa. Indy frowned. She was one of the gorgons from Greek mythology—half-human, half-creature, with live snakes for hair. Indy shivered just thinking about her. *Snakes*. They were the only thing he was afraid of.

"Believe me, lad, I know," Scythe said to Indy. "If we could find Markos Kourou, we would find the Pietroasa bowl. And, I daresay, many other stolen antiquities."

"Eric, I have a brilliant idea," Professor Jones said excitedly. "Junior and I will go to Greece!"

Indy's head snapped toward his father. Go to Greece to find Markos Kourou and the bowl? What a great idea! Indy couldn't believe it. His father never came up with great ideas like this.

Professor Jones noticed the look of surprise on Indy's face. He cleared his throat.

"Well," he said to his son, "I thought since Mr. Scythe can't make another replica until the real bowl is recovered, and since it was, in a way, your fault that the replica was smashed, we have an obligation to go after it."

"Absolutely right, Dad," said Indy.

"And I did promise you a short holiday before we go home to the United States," the professor went on, "now that your fall-term studies are over. So, we'll go to Greece and visit a former professor of mine named Nigel Wolcott. He lives in Athens."

"Why? I mean, who is he?" Indy asked.

"Nigel Wolcott was a brilliant lecturer at Oxford University. He was one of my teachers—one of my mentors, in fact. And he's a true scholar of Greek and Roman antiquities."

"You're going to find the bowl by *talking* about it, Dad?" Indy asked.

"Junior, someday you will realize that *research* is the key to discovering lost treasures," said Professor Jones. He looked happy, as if he had just passed on the meaning of life.

Oh, brother, Indy thought. You can *talk* about the Pietroasa bowl all you want, Dad. But I'm going to Athens to *find* it!

Chapter 2

The train swayed and clattered over the track as Indy stared out the window, watching the distant, craggy mountains of the Greek landscape pass by. He and his father had been traveling all night in the cramped third-class car. Now, in the morning sunlight, the land sparkled green from all the winter rains.

Just one more hour, Indy thought. Then we'll be in Athens and we can start looking for the thief no one has ever seen—Markos Kourou.

Indy's gaze moved to the two men sitting across from him. They looked like brothers, both in need of a shave and clean clothes. One carried a chicken in a wooden cage on his lap. The other carried a banged-up old guitar. They smiled. Indy smiled back.

Not much to say, guys, Indy thought. Especially since you speak only modern Greek—and I know only ancient Greek. And then Indy thought: How am I going to find the Pietroasa bowl if I can't speak the language?

Indy's father stirred next to him. "Where are we, Junior?" he asked, opening his eyes.

Indy stiffened. *Junior.* He hated that name, and his father knew it. "Dad, don't call me Junior!"

"Why not? It's your name. Henry Jones, Jr.," said Professor Jones.

"Oh, go back to sleep!" said Indy.

"I can't. I keep thinking about the bowl and how good it will be to see Nigel Wolcott again. He's an extraordinary scholar."

"Do you think he's ever seen the Pietroasa bowl?" Indy asked.

"I imagine he has. Why?"

"I was wondering what made it so special."

"Well, I didn't have much of a chance to look at it," Professor Jones said. "But as I recall, it depicts the Orpheus myth. Possibly the most tragic love story ever told. You remember the Orpheus story, don't you?"

"To tell you the truth, Dad, I've never been able to keep Orpheus straight."

"Why on earth not?"

"Don't you remember?" Indy said. "You insisted on telling me that story when I was sick as a dog with the flu. The whole time I was retching, you kept saying that a good Greek myth is the best medicine known to mankind. Anyway, all I remember about Orpheus is that he had something to do with the underworld."

"Well then, Junior, I'll have to tell you again, won't I?" Professor Jones said with obvious pleasure. He settled back in his seat and began the story. "Orpheus was a handsome young man who had a wonderful gift for music. He sang beautifully and he played a stringed instrument called the lyre. It was said that when Orpheus sang, birds stopped to listen and the gods wept."

"Oh!" Indy said. "Is he the one whose singing was so good, he was almost like a god?" His father nodded. "So what happened to him?"

"Well, one day Orpheus fell in love with a beautiful young woman named Eurydice. Soon they were married, but unhappily the marriage didn't last very long. Eurydice was bitten and killed by a snake."

Indy gave a small shudder. "Did it have to be a snake, Dad? I hate snakes."

"I have no control over the story, Junior. I didn't write it. It's thousands of years old."

"So is that the tragic part? Eurydice died?" said Indy.

"No, that's not the tragic part," said Professor Jones. "You see, Orpheus was so brokenhearted without Eurydice that he decided to go after her. He journeyed all the way to the underworld to beg its ruler, the god Pluto, to let Eurydice return to the world of the living.

"Of course the journey to the underworld was a difficult and dangerous one. Orpheus had to cross the river Styx—and that meant getting Charon, the ferryman, to take him across. He had to confront the horrible giant dog, Cerberus, who guarded the gates of the underworld. And he had to face the lord of the underworld himself. To say nothing of the fact that no mortal person had ever gone there before and returned alive."

Indy nodded. He knew that the underworld was a place of darkness and death in Greek mythology. Going there was no picnic.

"Well, Junior, Orpheus succeeded in all his tasks. He charmed the dog Cerberus with his song. And he even sang for Pluto, who fell under the spell of Orpheus's beautiful voice. 'You may take back your wife,' Pluto told Orpheus. 'With one condition.'"

"The gods never make things easy, do they, Dad?" said Indy.

Professor Jones shook his head. "Pluto told Orpheus he could leave the underworld and Eurydice would follow him. But he warned Orpheus *not to look back at her* until they had reached the world of the living."

"It sounds like a trick," Indy said.

"Well, Orpheus knew it was the only way to have Eurydice again, Junior. But when he had reached the living world, he couldn't hear her footsteps behind him and he began to doubt that she was there."

"There could have been a monster behind him. I'll bet he looked back," said Indy. "I would."

"That's exactly what Orpheus did," said Indy's father. "And with tragic results. You see, Eurydice *was* there, just a few steps behind, but she was still in the underworld. Orpheus wasn't supposed to look back until they were *both* outside. He saw her—but only for a second. Then she disappeared forever. Orpheus paid a terrible price for not doing what he was told."

"Sounds to me like he got tricked into making a bad deal," said Indy.

Professor Jones sighed and smiled. "Perhaps" was all he said.

Indy sat back in his seat and looked across the way. The two brothers had fallen asleep and were snoring loudly. Every so often the caged chicken squawked. The guitar rested on the seat beside the men. Just then the train lurched and the guitar tumbled onto the floor.

Indy bent over and picked it up. He strummed the guitar lightly a few times and some melodic chords rang out.

"Well, well, that is lovely, Junior," said Professor Jones. "Perhaps one day you'll be a musician, like Orpheus. Yes, that's it! You're my young Orpheus! From now on I'll call you Orpheus Junior. What do you think of that, Junior?"

"Don't call me *Junior*!" Indy grumbled as he put the guitar back on the seat.

Thirty minutes later the train pulled into the station in Athens.

It was an unusually warm day for January. Indy took off his coat and carried it over his arm. He and his father took a horse-drawn carriage through hilly streets to the home of Nigel Wolcott.

As they rode, Indy looked out at crowded stucco houses, mostly painted white. Grapevines grew in the yards of many houses and everyone seemed to have a dog. Along the way Indy saw ancient arches and temples with broken columns—pieces of buildings built more than two thousand years before. Near the heart of the city they passed an outdoor marketplace. Rugs, sheepskins, and colorful clothing were hanging everywhere.

The carriage stopped in front of a large yellow two-story stucco house set back slightly from the street. Around the windows were blue window sashes and shutters. In front there was a low stucco wall with a short wooden gate.

Indy's father went through the gate first. He led the way past some scrubby evergreen trees to a patio on the east side of the house. With the morning sun on it, the patio was the warmest place to be. There they found a man wrapped in a lap blanket, sitting on a chaise. He was eating black olives and spitting the pits onto the patio.

The man stood up as soon as he saw his visitors. He was a short, stocky man in his sixties wearing a tan suit, white shirt, bow tie, and flowing silk scarf. Under the shade of his wide-brimmed straw hat, his round face was soft and clean-shaven.

"Bless me a thousand times," he said in a surprised voice. "Is that really and truly you, Henry? Welcome, my boy, welcome."

Indy smiled. It was funny hearing someone call his father "boy."

Professor Jones shook hands with the old man. "It's so good to see you again, Nigel."

"And who is this handsome young man?" asked Nigel, giving Indy a gentle handshake. Indy noticed that Nigel's blue eyes were watery and moist. "Take off your hat and turn around, boy."

Indy didn't like to take off his hat, and he felt silly turning around for a stranger, like a little kid. But he did it. Anything to please the guy who might lead them to the Pietroasa bowl.

"He has his mother's fair looks," Nigel Wolcott said. "And he follows directions rather well. What's his name, Henry?"

"I like to be called Indiana, sir," Indy said.

The old man raised an eyebrow. "You mean, like one of your colonies?" he asked.

"Uh, states, sir," said Indy. "We call them states."

"Of course you do," Nigel said with a wry laugh. "I'm afraid that we Brits haven't entirely gotten used to that idea."

On the sunny patio, Nigel arranged three chairs and asked Indy and Professor Jones to sit while he went into the house. A few minutes later he returned with three glasses of lemonade on a silver tray.

"Now what brings you two to Athens?" asked Nigel. "Your telegram didn't say."

Indy's father explained about the damaged Pietroasa bowl. Then he told Nigel that the real bowl had been stolen.

"It's such a beautiful story," said Nigel, shaking his head contentedly.

Huh? Indy had never heard anyone describe a robbery that way.

"I mean, of course, the Orpheus legend," Nigel said. He spit out another olive pit.

"My dad says that maybe you can help us find the stolen bowl," said Indy.

"I'll do everything I can," Nigel said.

"Great," said Indy. He moved his chair in closer to Nigel. "We're pretty sure the thief is here in Athens."

"Well, let's not rush things. Let's start at the very beginning," Nigel Wolcott said slowly. "The Pietroasa bowl is one I'm familiar with. It was made sometime during the third century A.D. Of course it was named for the town in Rumania where it was discovered in 1837."

Professor Jones settled back in his chair, but Indy squirmed. Now we're going to hear a long lecture about the bowl, Indy thought. But when are we actually going to get busy and *find* it?

"Sir, we were hoping that you could tell us something about Markos Kourou," Indy said.

A look of surprise flashed across Nigel Wolcott's face. In the next instant, he picked up his glassful of lemonade and threw it at Indy—splashing him in the face!

Chapter 3

Indy sat stunned and sticky, his shirt and face soaked. The thick lemonade dripped onto his lap from the brim of his hat.

What's going on? Indy wondered. I mention Kourou and he throws lemonade in my face?

"Don't worry, my boy," Nigel said. "I scared it away."

"Scared *what* away?" asked Indy.

"The spider. Rather a big sort, too, crawling on the boy's neck," Nigel explained to Professor Jones.

Indy stood up and took a step back, his eyes searching the ground. Something black about the size of a quarter scurried away from his chair.

Oh, brother, Indy thought. A whole glass of lemonade just to chase off one little spider? If the spider had been any bigger, he probably would have thrown a chair!

"Thank you, Nigel," said Professor Jones.

"Uh, right. Thanks a lot, sir," said Indy.

The old man beamed. "Oh, we're friends now, young man. Don't be so formal. You may call me Professor Wolcott."

Professor Wolcott? Sure—that's real informal, thought Indy.

"Uh, Professor Wolcott, may I go wash up? I think I'm beginning to attract flies."

"Of course," Nigel said. "You'll find a washroom just inside the house."

Great, Indy thought, leaving the garden quickly. At least now he'd be on his own for a moment. He found a small room that smelled of dried wildflowers. A pitcher of water and a large bowl sat on a wooden washstand. Indy splashed his face, then took a clean shirt from one of the suitcases he and his father had brought. Suddenly he saw an envelope lying among his father's shirts.

It was the letter addressed to Eric Scythe, from his friend in Rumania.

Interesting, Indy thought. But why had Eric Scythe given it to his father? Maybe there was a clue in it. And of course his dad hadn't even bothered to tell him about it.

Typical, Indy thought as he picked up the envelope, took out the folded paper, and began to read.

"My dear Eric. How sad I am to write to you with news so terrible my hand trembles to set it down. The precious Pietroasa bowl has this week been stolen from my care.

"The thief was the one whose name is most cursed by you and me, the one with the Medusa-head cane. One person swore he saw the cane that day, but none saw the face of the villain who carries it.

"For now, I have kept the theft a secret, even from the directors. I am writing also to a police officer I have learned of. His name is Ari Naxakis; he lives in Athens and has sworn himself to find Kourou. His house is at Leanidou 73. I write about him because you are now his brother, the only two men I have told about this great tragedy and loss.

"Dear friend Eric, the replica bowl in your museum is now the only one the world may see. Guard its safety at all costs.

"Yours in sad friendship, Petrov."

I've got news for you, Dad, Indy thought as he slipped the letter into his pocket. Ari Naxakis is the man who should be helping us find the bowl. Not Nigel Wolcott!

As he walked back toward the patio, Indy heard Nigel saying, "You know, Henry, 1867 to 1868 was a most significant period in the history of the Pietroasa bowl. It was during this time that while on loan to the British Museum, an exact replica was produced."

Uh-oh. This guy's only up to 1867, Indy thought. He's still got forty-seven years to go before he even gets to the robbery! And Dad's in no hurry either.

Quickly a plan started to form in Indy's mind. Was it a crazy plan? Maybe. But listening to a twelve-hour history lesson sounded a lot crazier. Indy wanted facts—and that meant finding Ari Naxakis. Quietly he reversed his steps and slipped out the gate into the streets of Athens.

Now what? Indy wondered. He knew Ari Naxakis's address. The only thing he didn't know was how to get there, where he was right now, or how to speak Greek. Sure—he could probably read the street names since he knew the Greek alphabet. But ask for directions? Impossible.

With the letter gripped in his hand, Indy walked the streets of Athens, stopping people to show them the address of the police officer. Sometimes they pointed in reply. But mostly they shrugged to show that they didn't know—or couldn't read.

This is hopeless, Indy thought after an hour had passed. He had arrived at a narrow side street lined with small, two-story stucco buildings. The street sign said ΛΕΑΝΙΔΟΥ. Indy examined it—and nearly shouted for joy. It was Leanidou Street! He hurried toward number 73 and knocked eagerly on the door. There was no answer.

Indy knocked again. "Hello! Is anybody home?" he called.

A gruff voice on the other side of the door called back. It was a Greek reply, and Indy had no idea what it meant. But he opened the door and stepped into a room with a low ceiling and dim light from a single window. The room seemed to be a rustic kitchen. On one side was a small, cold fireplace, and along the other was a rough wooden table with two chairs. The middle of the floor was left open. No one was there.

"Hello? Who's here?" Indy called, taking a few more steps toward the back of the room.

Then, slowly, Indy stepped through an archway into an adjoining room. At first it, too, seemed to be empty except for several tall wooden chairs pushed to the side along the wall.

But then Indy saw him. A man in his fifties in a wheelchair, sitting in the middle of the room, aiming a pistol at Indy's heart.

The man looked surprised when he saw Indy.

"You? But you're just a boy!" the man said in English with a heavy Greek accent. He lowered the gun. "What are you doing here, young American?"

"I'm looking for Ari Naxakis," Indy said. "Do you know where he is?"

The man's upper lip twitched as he stared at Indy with dark eyes. But his expression remained stone cold. He was a big, broad man and seemed barely to fit in the wheelchair. His bushy mustache was gray and black, and so was his uncombed hair.

"He is dead," the man said. "A bullet in the back."

"Oh no." Indy's face filled with disappointment.

"But who sent you to look for him here?" the man asked.

"Someone in Rumania. Petrov," Indy replied.

When the man heard the name, his eyes opened wide.

"How do you know Petrov?" he asked. "What did he tell you of me?"

"Of you?" Indy asked. "But you're—"

"I'm no one." The man spit out the words.

But Indy shook his head and took off his hat. "No. You're Ari Naxakis!" he said. "You *must* be. You're the one person in the whole city of Athens who can help me!"

The man frowned. "Help you do what?"

"Help me find Markos Kourou."

Indy explained about Eric Scythe, the smashed replica of the Pietroasa bowl, and his quest for the thief of the original bowl.

But when Indy was done, Naxakis just shook his head.

"Go away, boy," Naxakis said. "I'm not looking for anyone now."

"But Kourou took a bowl that belongs in a museum!" Indy said.

"Bowls, chalices, paintings, statues, holy crucifixes. The man steals *everything*. Everything people hold dear." Naxakis waved the gun wildly as he gestured with his hand. "So best of fortune to you, my young friend."

"But how can you give up? You're a policeman," Indy said.

"I *was* a policeman. Now I'm just a crippled old fool," Naxakis said. "I made the mistake of getting too close to Kourou. I underestimated what a monster he is. Last year a bullet in the back changed everything—a bullet fired on Kourou's orders. You see how he steals everything people hold dear? Now go. Go while you can still walk."

Naxakis stared at Indy. But Indy didn't move, didn't blink.

"Why don't you go?" the man demanded.

"I can't," Indy said. "I need your help. You know about Kourou, but I don't. And I have legs, but you don't."

"And you think you're clever enough to find a man whose face no one has seen? A

man who eluded my grasp for ten years?"
Naxakis said. "Okay, then, tell me. How
would you go about finding Kourou?"

"I'd do whatever you'd do," Indy said.
"What would *you* do, Mr. Naxakis?"

"Call me Ari," the man said gruffly. He
put his gun away. Then he smiled and
pulled at his mustache. "Let me see. The
bowl is recently stolen. News of it will just
be reaching the antiquities shops in Athens.
I'd go to the shops for information."

"Which ones?" Indy asked.

Ari thought for a moment. Then he
wheeled over to a table against the wall. He
quickly wrote something on a piece of
paper, which he brought to Indy.

Indy could see it was a list with Greek let-
ters and numbers. Probably addresses. But
he had no idea where these places were.

"You can't read Greek, can you?" Ari cried
with a laugh. "Great detective!"

"I can read ancient Greek," Indy said.

Ari's face changed. "Ancient Greek? Really? Where do you come from, boy?"

"New Jersey," said Indy.

"Elyse! Elyse!"

What did I do now? Indy thought. *Does New Jersey mean something insulting in Greek?*

"Elyse!" Ari called once more.

A door creaked in another part of the house. A moment later a young woman of about twenty walked into the room. She was thin, with high cheekbones, and her long, straight hair matched the color of her shawl—black. But she was also wearing a long white skirt with colorful embroidery.

"Elyse," Ari said to her with a chuckle, "this boy is from New Jersey and he reads ancient Greek. And he's going to find Kourou!"

She gave Naxakis a puzzled but excited look. "That's wonderful, Father," she said.

Indy stared at her and smiled, until he felt a light slap on his face.

"Hey. Don't stare at her," Ari said. "This is my daughter."

"Hello," she said in a voice that sounded like a mellow flute. "Do you really think you can find Markos Kourou?"

"Ha!" Ari interrupted with a laugh. "He doesn't know the first thing about being a detective!"

"But I found you," Indy quickly pointed out. "And as for finding my way around Athens, your daughter could help me."

Ari's head turned sharply in his daughter's direction. "Out of the question," he snapped. "Do you think I'd let her do anything dangerous? One look at me will tell you Kourou's a maniac."

Elyse went to her father and hugged his neck. "What is so dangerous about showing a stranger our beautiful Athens?" she asked sweetly. "Tell me and I'll listen."

Ari was silent for a moment. He stroked his mustache with his open hand, but Indy could see a smile beginning to spread underneath.

"Perhaps you *could* find Kourou," he finally said. "But I am warning you: be careful with my daughter."

"Don't worry. I'm pretty good at dealing with trouble," Indy said.

"Trouble? You'd better not find any trouble. This is my daughter! If something happens to her, I'll rip out your throat with my own hands! Now go." With that Ari gave Indy a push. "Your journey begins."

Before Ari could change his mind, Indy

and Elyse hurried out the door. "By the way, my name's Indiana. Indiana Jones," he said when they were outside.

"Hello, Indiana Jones," she said.

"Does your father always talk so tough?" Indy asked.

"That was not tough," Elyse said proudly. "You should hear him when he is really angry at someone."

Just then a large black bird swooped down and landed on Indy's shoulder.

"Oh no!" Elyse cried, backing away.

"Hey, what's wrong?" Indy asked. "It's only a bird."

"No, it's not," Elyse said. "It's much worse. It's the raven of death!"

Chapter 4

The black bird hunched motionlessly on Indy's shoulder as if it were posing for a picture.

"What do you mean, it's the raven of death?" Indy asked, laughing.

"We do not laugh at gods and omens in Greece," said Elyse. "If you were Greek, you would understand."

"Understand what?" Indy asked.

"In Greek lore, the raven symbolizes death," she said. "It's a bad omen."

"In America when a bird lands on your shoulder, it just means you're going to get a messy shoulder," Indy said.

"This is not America," she answered.

Her voice sounded so serious that it stopped Indy for a moment. Did she really mean she wouldn't go with him because of a bird? "No, it's not America," Indy finally said. "It's Athens—where Markos Kourou lives. And I'm going to find him even if a whole flock of birds follows me everywhere. Are you going to help me?"

For a moment, she considered Indy's words. "My father says that being afraid and being brave feel the same in your head. But they feel different in your heart. And my heart tells me to help you." She waved her arm to chase the bird away. When it was out of sight, she said, "Let's go."

The route to the antiquities shops led them through several long blocks to a large, open-air marketplace known as the Plaka. When they had crossed it, they came to another narrow, shady street filled with houses, shops, and *tavernes*, or small cafés. Some of the shops were part of private houses, with goods displayed in the front room.

Indy followed Elyse into the first place on her father's list, a small, clean room with a wood plank floor. He looked around. There wasn't much for sale. Only a few ancient pieces of pottery.

For several minutes, Elyse spoke with the

shop owner in Greek. Then she shook her head at Indy.

"Ask him about Kourou," Indy said.

But when the owner heard the name, he fell silent and refused to say another word.

The same thing happened in the next shop—and the next and the next. No one knew anything, no one could help. And when Indy said Kourou's name, no one would talk about him.

"I guess that's how it is with Kourou," Indy said when they were back on the street. "No one knows what he looks like. But everyone knows his name."

Elyse nodded. "My father learned his name from the criminals who buy and sell the treasures that Kourou steals. He forced them to tell him about everything—even the Medusa-head cane. But even they do not know how Kourou looks."

"It sounds like your father is a pretty good policeman," Indy said.

"Not good," Elyse snapped, as if she had been insulted. "The best!"

"You must love him very much," said Indy.

"Yes," she said with a sigh. "But now I

cannot look at him in that chair, so I walk. I walk for hours. My father thinks I walk because I am studying Athens. He does not know that everywhere I am looking for a cane with a gold Medusa head and the fiend who carries it."

Indy nodded quietly.

"There is still one place left on my father's list," Elyse said. "But it is a long walk. Shall we go?"

"We have to," said Indy. "I've got to find that bowl. Besides, my father's probably still listening to Nigel Wolcott. They won't miss me for hours."

The fifth shop was in a very quiet block, farther away from the bustle of the large marketplace. As soon as Indy opened the door, he sensed that something was different. Music spilled out into the street from the well-kept house.

Inside, a young woman just slightly older than Elyse sat in a tall wooden rocking chair, rocking in time to the music. The music came from a gramophone on a low table beside her. The gramophone's big brass horn gleamed, as did the brass crank.

This doesn't look like a shop, Indy

40

thought. But just as he was about to ask Elyse if they were in the right place, the music caught his ear.

"I know this piece," Indy said. "It's from an opera. *Pagliacci*, by Leoncavallo. My father likes it."

The young woman in the rocking chair smiled and petted the fat orange cat that lay in her lap. "American?" she asked with a Greek accent.

"Yes," Indy said, glad that she spoke English.

But the young woman said nothing else. Instead, she closed her eyes and let the music play.

"Let's go," Elyse whispered to Indy. "This is not a shop."

Indy nodded. There were no display shelves or tables in the place. Instead, it looked like an English drawing room. The wall to the right was lined with tall, dark wooden bookcases. A wood-framed sofa with a plump colorful cushion sat in front of that wall. A polished dining table with carved chairs was on the left. A large crystal vase sat in the middle of the table. It was set with plates and silver for lunch.

"Okay," Indy said, nodding to Elyse. "Let's go."

But as they started to move toward the door, the young woman lifted the gramophone arm from the record. "Are you lost?" she asked. "The only Americans who come to this neighborhood are lost." Her voice was sweet, and she spoke English more confidently than Elyse. Indy even thought he heard traces of an English accent.

"I think maybe we *are* lost," Elyse said with embarrassment. "We were looking for a shop selling ancient artifacts."

The woman smiled. "This is just such a shop," she said. On her pretty pale face her red lipstick looked even darker.

"Really? Could have fooled me," said Indy.

"So many fine things in the room, except you have nothing to sell," said Elyse.

"The owner likes to keep the shop this way," the young woman said. "It is safer. The antiquities are stored in the back."

She stood up, spilling the cat onto the floor, and gestured for them to sit. "My name is Kalitsa. Let me bring some refreshments. Then I will help you."

Indy sat down, but he was watching a thin golden curtain covering a doorway on the back wall. The curtain moved in the draft. Was the bowl back there? Indy wondered. The doorway seemed to lead to where the antiquities were kept.

Kalitsa went into the back. She returned a moment later bringing three glasses of water to the table. Balanced on the rim of each glass was a spoon with dark jelly in it.

"In Greece, this means good hospitality to a guest," Elyse explained to Indy. "Eat the jelly, put the spoon in the glass, and drink the water."

Indy followed Elyse and Kalitsa, eating the thick plum jelly and drinking the sweetened water.

"I'll bet you are looking for a book," said Kalitsa. "Americans are always looking for books."

"I'm looking for a bowl," said Indy. "It's gold, with figures of Orpheus and other Greek gods etched on it."

Kalitsa thought for a moment. "No. I have never seen such a bowl. It is not Greek, is it?"

Indy looked surprised. "No. But how did you know that?"

"The Greeks did not do much metal-work," she explained.

"Up until a few weeks ago, it was in Rumania," Indy said. "It was stolen by Markos Kourou."

Kalitsa frowned. "I'm sorry to hear that it has been stolen. Maybe you can come back and talk to the man who owns this shop." She picked up the cat and placed it on her lap again. "The owner is out of town until next week. He can help you more."

Indy nodded. But as he got up to leave, a breeze lifted the thin gold curtain on the back wall. Indy caught a glimpse of a hall-way beyond it. And out of the corner of his eye, he saw something that made his knees feel weak.

Resting against the hallway wall was a long ebony cane with a golden head of Medusa on top—just like the cane Markos Kourou carried!

Chapter 5

Indy forced himself not to look at the curtain.

Was that Kourou's Medusa-head cane? Or someone else's? And if it was Kourou's, what was it doing there? Was Kourou hiding in the back room watching them? If not, would he come back for it? And why had Kalitsa acted like she had never heard of him?

Indy's head was spinning with questions. But he tried to act calm. He sat down again casually and studied Kalitsa's face while she and Elyse spoke in Greek. She smiled as she stroked the orange cat. If she was in a hurry to get rid of them, he couldn't tell. There was nothing about her that made him think she was lying.

Except that she had the cane of a notorious thief in her back hall!

Kalitsa turned to Indy. "Indiana, I hear you are a young policeman, a man with a mission."

"Not exactly. I'm going to be an archeologist," Indy said. "But it's sort of the same thing sometimes."

Kalitsa tilted her head with interest. "I don't understand," she said.

"Well, when I'm looking for something, first I have to find a trail. And everyone leaves a trail—whether it's a thief or a whole civilization," Indy explained.

"Something tells me you will succeed, Indiana," Kalitsa said.

Indy nodded and said goodbye as casually as he could. A moment later, he and Elyse were on the street again.

Without saying a word, Indy walked to the end of the block, turned left, and then turned left again into a narrow alleyway.

"Where are you going? We are walking in circles," Elyse said. "This is not the way back."

"I know," said Indy, looking behind him to make sure no one was following. Then he

46

walked up to the door that led from the alley into the rear of Kalitsa's shop.

"I have to go back inside," he whispered. "Markos Kourou may be in there!"

"Kourou?" Elyse said the word slowly.

Indy wasn't sure why she believed him so quickly. Maybe because it was the thing she wanted to believe more than anything else. When he told her about the cane, her face filled with passionate hate.

"I'm going in with you!" Elyse insisted.

"No! I promised your father no danger."

"But it's Kourou." She said his name as if it were a curse. "Would you spit in his face?"

"Spit? Are you kidding?"

"That's why I'm going with you," Elyse said, and she reached for the door latch first.

As she opened the door a crack, Indy prayed someone had oiled the hinges some-time during the last century or so.

Together they peeked in the small open-ing. At least no one was in the back room. They opened the door farther and slipped inside. Freestanding wooden shelves were lined up along the walls. The musty smell of antiquity, a smell Indy knew so well, was heavy in the air.

Indy moved silently to the far end of the room and walked down the dark hallway toward the thin golden curtain. On the other side of it, Kalitsa was pacing in the front room. He watched her feet pass back and forth in front of the curtain. Elyse came up behind him in the hallway.

Propped against the wall in the hallway—just inches from his hand—was the golden-topped cane. Slowly Elyse reached for it, but Indy grabbed her wrist. Their eyes met. Hers were aflame, but Indy shook his head hard.

Kourou's cane was not what they were after. It was Kourou himself—and the bowl!

Quietly they moved back into the store-room and began to check all the shelves. Vases, pieces of statuary and friezes, plates and goblets—the shelves held old and valuable artifacts.

"Kourou must have been here," Elyse whispered, trembling with anger and looking at the cane.

"But the bowl isn't," Indy said. "We'd better go before Kalitsa finds us."

But just as they moved for the door, they heard a man's voice in the front room. Someone had come into the shop! He was speaking in Greek to Kalitsa.

"Kourou!" Elyse said. "It must be!"

Here? Now? Indy's heart began to pound.

"Stay by the door. Be ready to run," he whispered.

Then he inched his way down the dark hallway again, toward the gold curtain. He was standing so close to it that a hard breath would have puffed the thin material. He squinted and stared, hoping to get the first look at Markos Kourou that any of his opponents had ever had.

Kalitsa was standing with her back to the curtain, blocking Indy's view. He waited for her to move aside, but she seemed rooted to the floor.

"Meow." The orange cat brushed against the front of the curtain. Indy stepped back and held his breath, hoping the curtain wouldn't move.

Kalitsa finally turned sideways and took a step. But at the same time, so did the man. He was still out of Indy's line of sight. Indy decided to pull the edge of the curtain aside, just enough to peek out. He had to risk it. The chance to see Kourou was too good to miss.

But as he stepped another inch closer and touched the curtain, somehow his other hand knocked into the cane. It fell to the floor with an awful clatter.

Instinct took over. Every muscle in Indy's body said, "Get out—*now*!" He ran toward the back door, grabbing Elyse's arm as he passed her. Together they sprinted down the alley as fast as they could.

At the end of the alley, Indy looked back, just long enough to see a huge muscular man—was it Kourou?—racing toward them, shouting in Greek.

If that was Kourou, Indy thought, he was nothing like what Indy had expected. He was young and athletic. His clean-shaven, angular face was handsome. He had a full head of thick black curls. And he could run like the wind.

Indy and Elyse took off down the street— and suddenly found themselves heading downhill toward a plaza. Indy raced for a group of pushcarts filled with rugs, leather goods, and fruits and vegetables.

"Keep running no matter what!" he shouted to Elyse. Then he dropped to the ground and rolled under a huge pushcart filled with fruit. When Indy stood up again, he bumped his head hard on the cart.

"Ow!" he cried as he grabbed the cart handles and tipped the cart over. Oranges, figs, and lemons slid to the ground, rolling everywhere.

The man who was chasing them was running so fast he couldn't stop. He skidded on the fruit, tripped, and fell hard on his back.

Quickly Indy turned the cart all the way over on top of the man and then started running again. As he dashed off, he heard Kourou—or whoever it was—and the cart owner shouting curses in Greek.

"Elyse!" Indy called.

"Indiana!" Her voice rang out from the corner of a whitewashed building. "This way!"

Indy saw her pointing down a narrow alley that led away from the marketplace. Without waiting for him, she started running again, her sandals slapping loudly on the cobblestones.

Indy followed, almost letting out a sigh of

relief. Now all they had to do was reach the end of the alley and turn the corner. Then they would be out of Kourou's sight.

But halfway down the alley, he stopped dead. A rider mounted on a tall white horse had appeared at the end of the alley. His eyes coldly met Indy's.

"No," Indy said out loud. "It's impossible." He stood frozen. Elyse stopped in her tracks too. Out of the corner of his eye, Indy saw Elyse make the sign of the cross.

The rider shouted and kicked at his horse's flanks. Then the pure white stallion started galloping, its hooves banging on the cobbled street.

It can't be, Indy thought again. The rider charging on the horse was the same muscular man Indy had just buried under a pushcart of fruit!

There was nowhere to run now, nowhere to hide. Indy pushed Elyse toward a doorway. Then he stood firmly in the middle of the alley—as if waiting to be trampled to death!

Chapter 6

Indy watched the horse and rider charging down the narrow alleyway toward him.

Is Kourou some kind of magician? Indy wondered. How can he possibly lie under a pushcart one second and then ride a white horse the next?

When the stallion was only yards away, Indy frantically waved his hat in the air and yelled as loud as he could. Then he dropped to his knees.

Just as Indy had hoped, the horse started. It reared and threw the curly-haired Greek to the ground.

"Come on!" Indy called to Elyse.

She leaped from the doorway where she had been hiding. Breathless and terrified, they raced past the white horse and fallen rider to the far end of the alley. Indy knew it was only a matter of minutes before Kourou would be chasing them again.

They turned a corner and suddenly, in the near distance, Indy saw the most beautiful sight in all of Athens. It was the sacred hill, the Acropolis, with the ancient temple called the Parthenon at the top. The Parthenon had been built in the fifth century B.C. as a temple to the Greek goddess Athena. But Indy wasn't thinking about its historical importance or the beauty of the architecture. It just looked like a great place to hide—if only they could get there.

That's when he realized they were running toward a seven-foot-high stone wall at the far end of the street. They were trapped!

Now what? Indy wondered as they ran past a wooden donkey cart standing in front of a house. For a moment, Indy considered stealing the cart and trying to charge back right at Kourou. But then he saw something much better. A horsewhip!

Reaching into the cart, Indy grabbed the long whip and unfurled it with a snap.

Then he looked around for a target. A tall tree stood a few feet from the wall.

Perfect, Indy thought. Now if only I can get a good running start...

He backed up a few feet, then ran full speed ahead. When he had almost reached the tree, he cracked the whip and wrapped it around a high, thick branch.

In the next instant, holding tight to the whip, he gave a mighty leap. His body swung forward in a graceful arc that carried him all the way to the top of the wall.

"Come on! I'll pull you up!" he called to Elyse, just as Kourou came charging toward them on horseback once again.

Indy reached down, grabbed Elyse's arms, and helped her scramble up onto the wall.

"Nice try," Indy called, laughing at the desperate look on Kourou's face.

Indy flung the whip up into the tree, out of reach. Then he and Elyse dropped to the ground on the other side and ran up the slope of the Acropolis.

When they reached the Parthenon at the top, Indy fell down on the steps, breathing hard.

Elyse sat beside him. "Thank you," she said. "My father would be proud."

"Really?"

"Yes. But he would also rip your throat out for exposing his daughter to such dangers. So I won't tell him how brave you were."

Indy smiled as he lay back on the steps and looked at the view.

"You know where we are, don't you?" Elyse said. "This is the Acropolis. *Acropolis* means…"

Indy smiled to himself. He knew what *Acropolis* meant. This was the one part of Greece he knew very well—ancient Greece.

He had studied it all years before with his British tutor, Miss Seymour. And he had memorized all the important facts. That the Greeks first built a city here between 461 and 429 B.C., during the Golden Age of Greece. That they had chosen this location because of the many natural springs of water, and because the location on a hill was easy to defend from attack.

But seeing it now from the top, being here, he suddenly understood for the first time what it must have felt like to live in ancient times.

"*Acropolis*. It means 'High City,'" Indy said, interrupting Elyse.

She smiled warmly. "Do you hear the voices of the gods speaking to you, Indiana?"

"No, the voice of Miss Seymour—much stronger."

Elyse looked puzzled, but Indy was busy gazing at the Parthenon. It was even more beautiful up close, he thought. No wonder Miss Seymour called it the most perfect building in all the world. Its forty-six marble columns, once white, were now honey colored, chipped away by time and man. But they were still surprisingly regular—and they formed a shape that seemed to reach for the sky.

"Well, we finally saw Markos Kourou," said Elyse.

"Maybe. Maybe not," Indy said. "I keep asking myself one question. Why would a master thief with a secret identity chase us through the streets of Athens? It would give away his disguise."

"That's true," Elyse said reluctantly. "But for certain we saw the cane. Kourou *was* in the shop sometime. And Kalitsa lied to us. She said she knew nothing about Kourou and the golden bowl."

Before Indy could say anything else, an unmistakable sound made him sit up.

Tap-tap. Tap-tap.

It was a cane tapping on the marble stairs behind him.

Could it be Markos Kourou? Indy turned in alarm.

But it was only a small, frail woman coming from the Parthenon. She had white hair and a stooped back, and she rested her weight on a cane as she walked. Her long black dress and the black kerchief on her head made her look like a shadow against the late afternoon sky.

"Where'd she come from? We didn't see anyone there a few minutes ago," Indy said.

"*Kalímera*," the tiny old woman said, smiling at Elyse.

Indy, who learned new languages fast, had picked up some phrases in the shops that day. He knew that the old woman's greeting meant "Good afternoon."

Elyse returned the greeting as the woman stopped and stood in front of Indy.

The woman reached down and pinched Indy's cheek hard. "And good day to you, my little *loukániko*," she said, laughing.

Indy stood up and looked at Elyse. "What did she call me?"

"A sausage," said Elyse.

The old woman straightened her back as much as she could. But her wrinkled, leathery face came no higher than Indy's chest.

She pointed to one eye and then the other. "With my left eye, I see the past," she said in a scratchy voice. "With my right eye, I see the future."

Indy looked carefully. One eye was brown, one was green. They seemed to move independently of each other. "Okay," Indy said, smiling. "If you can see the past, what grade did I get on my last Latin test?"

That joke earned him a rap on the shoulder with her heavy black cane.

Turning her head to the side, the old woman fixed her left eye on Indy. "You have come here on a quest. You are looking for something," she said.

Indy felt Elyse's hand grip his arm.

"Go on," Elyse urged. "Please go on."

"I see an injury to your head," said the fortuneteller. With a swipe of her cane, she knocked Indy's hat off and felt the top of his head. Her shaky hand soon discovered the lump from bumping his head on the fruit cart.

Indy was silent. At least the old woman was putting on a good show.

"Now what can you tell us about the future?" Elyse asked quickly.

The old woman's right eye twitched as she stared at Indy. But she said nothing.

"What do you see?" Elyse asked, touching the old woman's arm.

"Yeah, tell us," said Indy.

"The past is free," croaked the fortune-teller. "The future will cost you."

"I don't have any money," Indy said.

"I know," said the old woman, looking up into Indy's face. "But that is not the cost I mean."

She seemed to be daring him to ask. So Indy took the dare.

"Tell me, please," he said. "What do you see?"

"I see you walking in the paths of the gods," she said, closing her eyes. "Even if you do not wish it, you will relive the life of a hero. But you will also descend...down... down...into the depths of danger...and death!"

Chapter 7

"Walk in the paths of the gods...into the depths of danger...and death."

Indy heard the old woman's words over and over as if she had planted her strange, raspy voice in his brain. He stepped in front of her to block her way. "What does someone have to do to get a good omen around here?" he said.

She raised a hand that smelled of olives and rosemary and ran dry, bent fingers down Indy's face. "Little *loukániko*," she said. "I didn't want to tell you."

"You haven't told me anything," Indy said.

The old woman pursed her cracked lips and looked at Elyse. "I can see I have told you too much."

"Please," begged Elyse. "Tell us what your visions mean. You must."

"It wouldn't matter, child," said the old woman. "When you walk in the paths of the gods, you can only follow one road. All heroes know this."

Indy felt himself shiver. The last thing in the world he wanted to do was believe this old woman. But she seemed to know things...

"I must go," she said, moving Indy aside with a wave of her cane. "You must go too." She took a few limping steps and then, turning, she raised a palm to keep them from following. But as she walked down the steps to the stony path, she stumbled suddenly. The cane fell from her frail hand.

Indy hurried to pick it up. The black ebony wood felt heavy in his hands. But it was the top that caught his eye. Its *gold* top! It had been hidden by the long, full sleeve of her dress, but now Indy saw that the handle was beautifully sculpted gold—exactly as on Markos Kourou's cane! Except that the top was not a three-dimensional head of Medusa. It was a young man carrying a sword and shield.

"Where did you get this cane?" Indy asked excitedly. He held it up but didn't give it back to the fortuneteller.

"Why do you ask?" she said in a crackly voice.

"What is it, Indiana?" asked Elyse.

"A good omen," Indy said with a laugh. "Look. It's the same kind of cane as Kourou's."

"And look at the handle!" Elyse said. "It is Perseus, the Greek hero who killed the snake-haired Medusa!"

Indy dangled the cane in front of the old woman. "Where did you get it?" he asked again.

"I don't remember," she answered haltingly.

"Maybe if you look at it with your left eye, you'll remember," Indy said.

The old woman quickly snatched her cane. "The canemaker lives by the water," she said.

The water? Why did she say that word as if it were a threat?

"Where?" asked Elyse. "Give us the address."

"Akti Koundourioti," the old woman said. "In Piraeus. His name is Charon." Then without another word she hurried away and disappeared down the hill of the Acropolis.

Indy listened to the tap of her cane as he fished in his pocket for a piece of paper and wrote down the canemaker's name and address.

"The same man made both of those canes," Indy said. "I'm almost sure of it. Maybe he can lead us to Kourou."

"But you heard what the old woman saw in your future. Indiana, aren't you afraid?" Elyse asked.

"I've got to follow the trail," he said.

The dark shadows of the Parthenon were lengthening. The sun's light was changing from yellow to blood red. Through the Acropolis, the late afternoon sunset cast an eerie glow.

For the first time in hours, Indy thought about his father and Nigel Wolcott. "It's getting late," Indy said. He began to walk down the hill. "I guess I'll have to check out the canemaker tomorrow."

"*You* will?" asked Elyse. "And are you thinking you can find him without a guide?"

"But you saw what happened today," Indy said. "The closer we get to Kourou, the more dangerous it becomes. And I promised your father we wouldn't do anything dangerous. How are you going to explain any of this to him without making him angry?"

"That's easy," Elyse said. "I will not explain it! Do you think I want him to worry? Ha! Instead, I will tell him that we had a pleasant day today. And tomorrow you asked me to show you the wonderful craftsmen of Athens. Then we will go to the canemaker and my father will not object. Especially if I make him *fasólada* for dinner. Bean soup is his favorite."

"Whatever you say." Indy gave in with a shrug.

As they left the Acropolis, dusk was settling in. Indy looked carefully in every direction. Was it safe to leave? Was anyone waiting to follow them or chase them again?

A small horse-drawn cab was parked just outside the wall that surrounded the Acropolis, down the street from the entrance gate. A lone cab waiting for the last visitors to the Parthenon, which Indy and Elyse seemed to be.

"Let's not walk. That carriage will be safer," Indy said, leading Elyse across the rocky ground.

The white carriage horse kept its head down, nibbling the dry grass. The driver, wearing a shirt with a hood, seemed to be asleep. He didn't even turn around as Indy handed Elyse up into the back seat of the small open carriage.

But once she was inside, the driver suddenly stood up. At first, all Indy saw was the long, stiff driver's whip in his raised hand. But then the hood fell back and he saw the man's face. Not again! Indy thought. It was the muscular, curly-headed Greek who had chased them from Kalitsa's shop!

As Indy climbed up and tried to pull Elyse from the carriage, the whip came down sharply on his shoulder. Indy jerked in pain and instantly fell back onto the cobblestones. Quickly the driver turned and whipped his large white horse. With a shout and a clatter, the carriage bolted away.

"Indiana!"

It was Elyse's cry that Indy heard over the calls of the driver and the crack of the whip.

"Indiana! Help!"

Oh no! Indy thought as the horrible truth sank in. The man was kidnapping Elyse!

Chapter 8

"Wait! Elyse! Stop!" Indy cried, jumping to his feet and chasing the carriage.

The driver snapped his whip, yelling at the horse to go faster. Elyse looked back in horror, bouncing with the wild ride.

Indy ran until his sides ached, but there was nothing he could do to stop the carriage from disappearing into the tangled web of Athens' streets.

"Walk in the paths of the gods?" Indy angrily shouted the words of the fortune-teller. "Relive the life of a hero?" What a joke! The laugh that came out of him was cruel and desperate. How was he ever going to tell Ari Naxakis that his daughter had been kidnapped?

Darkness was smothering the houses when Indy reached Ari Naxakis's neighborhood. Only a bit of light flickered in the small front window of Ari's house.

Indy knocked. No answer. He opened the front door and stepped in. "Mr. Naxakis?" Indy called.

Ari was in one corner of the living room, sleeping in his wheelchair by a table with a dimly lit oil lamp. His head was slumped forward; a book was open on his lap.

"Ari," Indy called again.

This time the man woke up. His large dark eyes met Indy's. It seemed to take him a few seconds to remember.

"Where is Elyse?" he asked quietly.

"She's..." Indy began to tremble.

"Where!" Ari said, raising his voice.

"She's been kidnapped, maybe by Kourou." Indy said it quickly to get it over with.

Pain showed on Ari's large face. Then anger seemed to twist all of his features. "Kidnapped!" he yelled, throwing his book at Indy. His massive hands grabbed at the large wheels of his wheelchair, trying to propel himself at the boy. But he used too much force and leaned too far out. With a loud crash, he fell onto the floor and the chair skidded away behind him. "Kourou?

Elyse! I'll kill you!" From the floor he lifted himself onto his elbows and shouted like a madman.

Indy took a step backward. "I'm sorry. I—" Then he watched Ari begin to drag himself, drag his lifeless legs and heavy body across the floor by his brawny arms.

"I'm going to kill you with my bare hands," said Ari, gasping with painful effort. "Try to run, but I'll find you."

Indy knew that somehow he could get his trembling legs to run away, but he didn't want to. "I'm not going to run," he said. "I came here first because I thought we could do something to help her."

"Why didn't you stop him?" demanded Ari, creeping closer.

"Don't you think I tried!" Indy shouted back.

Ari stopped. He buried his head in his crossed forearms and wept on the floor.

A few minutes passed before the house fell silent. Indy retrieved the wheelchair and helped Ari back into it.

"Go home," Ari said, his voice softer but sadder. "It's not your fault. It is Kourou. No one can defeat him."

"But I'm not giving up," said Indy. "And you can't either. Come with me to the house where my father is staying. Maybe he and his friend will be able to help."

"Help?" Ari said with a contemptuous laugh. He grabbed Indy's shirt. "Don't you understand yet? If Elyse has fallen into Markos Kourou's hands, she might as well have entered the underworld. Only Orpheus could bring her back!"

Indy pulled away from him, almost tearing his own shirt. "Orpheus?" he said. He remembered what his father had called him on the train—Orpheus Junior. "You'll walk in the paths of the gods," Indy said out loud.

"What are you talking about?"

"Relive the life of a hero," Indy said. He couldn't believe what he was thinking. "Maybe that's what people have been trying to tell me. Maybe I *am* Orpheus. If so, then I can bring Elyse back—even if I have to go to the underworld to do it!"

Ari shook his head as if now he felt more alone than ever. But Indy ignored him. He bundled the old man up warmly. Then he explained everything to Ari as he pushed his wheelchair through the streets to Nigel Wol-

70

cott's house. On the way, they stopped to report the kidnapping to the police. Ari translated as Indy told the police about the antiquities shop, the Greek man on horse-back, and even about seeing Kourou's cane.

"You know nothing," said Ari afterward.

Maybe so, Indy thought. Maybe not.

Nigel's house was brightly lit when they arrived, and music was coming from it. Someone was playing the piano.

Indy brought Ari into the entryway of the house, where they were met by Nigel. He was now dressed in an Edwardian dinner jacket and ruffled shirt.

"Oh, Henry, your prodigal son has re-turned," Nigel called into the living room. His watery blue eyes sparkled as he clapped his hands with a sort of excited delight. "You gave us a bit of a start, young man, once we finally realized you weren't here."

Professor Jones came from the living room as the piano music continued.

"Junior, you're here at last," said Profes-sor Jones, with a slight note of annoyance in his voice. "We've been waiting dinner."

"Dad—and Professor Wolcott—this is Ari Naxakis," Indy said. "He's the policeman

71

who's been looking for Kourou for ten years."

As Indy's father and Nigel shook hands with Ari, Indy noticed that the piano music had stopped. A fat orange cat came from the living room and trotted stiff-legged toward Indy. He watched the cat rubbing against his legs, and when he looked up, a woman was standing in the archway to the living room. It was Kalitsa—the young woman from the antiquities shop!

Indy was speechless.

"Oh, Miss Tstouris, this is my son, Henry Junior," said Professor Jones.

"I thought his name was Indiana," she said with a smile, picking up her cat.

"What are you doing here?" Indy blurted out. Only his father's stare reminded him that he was being rude.

"Kalitsa is the wife of a very good friend of mine, the dear girl," said Nigel. "Unfortunately my friend couldn't be here tonight."

Oh, great, Indy thought. Why hadn't Nigel mentioned that he knew someone who worked in an antiquities shop? The man was useless. Utterly useless!

"And where is *your* friend?" asked Kalitsa, giving Indy a warm smile.

"My daughter has been kidnapped," Ari answered stonily.

Kalitsa put her hands to her face. "How dreadful," she said.

"Maybe by Markos Kourou," said Indy. "I asked Mr. Naxakis to come because we've got to do something to help."

"Quite horrible," Professor Jones said. "Have you gone to the police?"

"We did before we came here, Dad," said Indy. Then he told his father everything that had happened.

"Well, why don't we all go in to dinner and put our heads together?" Nigel suggested. "Do stay and join us, won't you, Mr. Naxakis? Although I daresay dinner conversation is going to be glum."

Nigel guided Ari and Kalitsa to the dining room, but Indy held his father back.

"Dad, do you think it's possible to relive the Orpheus legend?"

"I relive it frequently, Junior," his father answered with a smile. "I relive it in my head."

73

Indy lowered his voice even more. "I mean in real life, Dad," he said.

"In real life?" Professor Jones laughed. "Junior, have you been hit on the head?"

"At least once today, actually—yes," said Indy.

The dinner was delicious—stuffed grape leaves, lamb casserole, and other Greek foods served on fine china at a long, dark, polished wooden table. Two large golden candelabra lit the table brightly, while gas lamps along the walls lighted the room's many antiques.

But Indy couldn't eat more than a bite. He took only one purple fig from a blue-painted bowl on the table and could hardly swallow the soft, sweet fruit. How could he eat when so much had gone wrong? First the Pietroasa bowl was lost. Now Elyse.

Instead, Indy watched Ari, who looked sad with his grief and uncomfortable with the finery in the room. He also watched Kalitsa. She smiled when he caught her eye, and again when he caught her sneaking a bite of food to the cat in her lap.

"A man chased me from your store this afternoon," Indy said. "Who was he?"

Kalitsa laughed. "Was that you?" she said. "He was a customer. I don't know who he was. He heard a noise and said, 'I think you're being robbed.' Then he ran into the back room to help."

"He was the man who kidnapped Elyse," Indy said.

"No! What were you doing behind the store?" asked Kalitsa.

"I wanted to look at a cane that was hidden behind the curtain, a cane with a golden Medusa head."

Indy noticed that he now had his father's complete attention. Nigel, however, was busy enjoying his soup.

"A customer left that cane weeks ago," said Kalitsa.

"What was his name?" Indy asked.

"But I don't know," Kalitsa said. "I had never seen him before and have never seen him since. Since he did not come back, I thought the cane must not be very important to him."

"It is very important to him," Ari said.

"Tell us, dear girl," said Nigel. "What did he look like? This is exciting."

Kalitsa closed her eyes and tried to

remember. "He was about forty years old," she said. "His hair was sandy brown and fine. He had a scar like a small lightning bolt on one cheek, and I think he walked with a limp. I was surprised he did not return for his cane."

"You have seen Markos Kourou!" said Ari. "Ha! He has a face. He makes mistakes. He is a man after all!"

"But he's not the guy who kidnapped Elyse," Indy said. "That guy had dark hair."

Kalitsa's eyes danced even brighter. "I just remembered something he said. He didn't say where, but I think he mentioned living in a small town in the hills ten miles north of Athens."

"That's where you must go, boy—first thing in the morning," Ari said, pointing to Indy. "To find Kourou and Elyse."

"Is this the trail you've been looking for?" asked Kalitsa.

Indy nodded. The facts made sense. At least they seemed to. That Kourou would want to hide outside of Athens in a small village. That when he came to Athens, he would visit a shop away from the crowds and out of sight.

But still something was troubling Indy. If Indy was really following in Orpheus's footsteps, should he be traveling *north* up into the sunny mountains of Greece? Was that the path *down*—to find the terrible god of the underworld?

Chapter 9

Early the next morning, Indy rushed into the dining room in Nigel Wolcott's house. The room was beginning to glow with early morning sun.

"Dad, who is Charon?" Indy asked.

"Charon?" his father repeated. He laid a bookmark across the page he was reading and closed his book. Then he picked up his cup of tea from the breakfast table and took a thoughtful sip.

Why was it every time Indy started talking twice as fast, his father started reacting twice as slow?

"I was getting ready for the trip into the hills to look for Kourou," Indy said. "And then I found this paper in my pocket with the name of the canemaker on it. Charon. It sounds familiar."

"Come now, Junior," his father coaxed. "Think of the Orpheus legend."

"Good morning, chaps." Nigel came into the room behind Indy and greeted them in a bright red silk dressing gown. "My, you two are early birds. I thought we might go down to the market for some coffee and rolls."

"Dad, this is important! Who is Charon?"

"You two are always quizzing each other, aren't you?" Nigel said. "Do you mind if I join in? I'll bet I could come up with some challenging questions."

I'm going to strangle this guy with his red silk belt if he doesn't shut up, Indy thought. Doesn't anyone care that a girl has been kidnapped?

"Charon was the mythological ferryman who took people across the river Styx to the underworld," Professor Jones stated. "Remember?"

"Did he take Orpheus, Dad?"

"Yes, he did. But of course Orpheus had to charm him first."

"Then you know what, Dad? I'm not going to the hills to look for Kourou. I'm going to find this man Charon. Because that's what Orpheus did."

"The boy sounds positively superstitious, Henry," Nigel said with concern. "That's not very scholarly."

"Professor Wolcott," Indy said, "can you tell me how to get to Piraeus? The cane-maker lives there."

Nigel shook his head with a wry smile. "I'm afraid I'm not the one to ask," he said. "I followed a map once. I got to Wales. Of course I was trying to get to France."

"That's okay. Thanks. I'll find it," Indy said, hurrying to the front door.

"But where are you off to, lad?"

"I'm going to find Eurydice," Indy said.

Nigel and Indy's father looked puzzled.

"I mean, Elyse."

Out on the street, Indy hired a carriage and asked the driver to take him to the address the old woman had given him. "Piraeus," Indy said, hoping that the driver nodded because he understood.

The ride was slow, dusty, cold, and long, but about an hour later the driver called out "Piraeus." He pointed to the city that was coming into view. With its factories and run-down houses, it was smaller and gloomier than Athens. But Indy didn't mind.

The gloom made it seem more like the underworld—and that's where Indy wanted to go.

As the carriage rolled downhill to the harbor, Indy looked out and saw beautiful blue-green water. It was really the Aegean Sea, but to Indy it seemed like the river Styx. Small fishing boats with stiff white sails stood out against distant rocky islands.

The carriage stopped in front of a shack set back from the docks. Indy paid the driver and climbed out.

As he approached the shack, Indy heard the sound of a machine inside and a man's voice, half-humming, half-moaning. An old man was bent over a lathe, carving a spinning piece of wood. Wood shavings flew everywhere and fell on him like snow.

Indy knocked at the opening to the shop. The old man stopped his work and stared out. He kept a clay pipe clamped in the corner of his mouth.

"Omilíte angliká?" said Indy, asking if the man spoke English.

The man nodded silently and looked suspiciously at Indy.

"Are you the canemaker Charon?"

"Both are my fate," he said, his clay pipe still in his mouth. He was very old, and the skin on his bony frame was wrinkled. But he stood up straight, watching Indy through sparkling eyes. Wood chips stuck to him everywhere.

"I saw two of your canes yesterday," said Indy.

"Why would a boy come this long way to talk about canes?" the old man asked.

"I met an old woman who had a cane with a golden Perseus head. Do you remember it?"

Indy expected the old man to smile or nod or react in some way. But he didn't. Instead, he walked past Indy to a barrel of water that stood outside the doorway. The man leaned forward and plunged his face into it, coming up dripping wet but free of the wood chips. Then without a word, he walked back into his workshop.

Indy couldn't tell if his silence meant hostility or fear. "The other cane had a gold Medusa head," Indy said. "That's the one I'm interested in."

The old man's eyes squinted coldly as he leaned with his forearms against the doorway. Even in old age his arms looked powerful. "I have made canes for sixty years," he said, his voice rough. "Why do you want me to remember this one?"

"The Medusa-head cane is special to me," said Indy. "The man who owns it is a thief."

"What has he stolen of yours?" Charon asked.

"Nothing of mine," Indy said. "But he's stolen things that belong to everyone. And yesterday he took something that no one could replace. I have to get her back."

Charon puffed on his pipe and shook his head. He started moaning and muttering again. "Could it be a Medusa head on an ebony stick?" he said finally.

Indy smiled. "Yes, that's the one. Do you remember the man who bought it?"

Charon shrugged. "Not his name or his face. I never saw him. The cane was ordered by someone who worked for him. I delivered it to his house more than fifteen years ago."

"Then you remember where he lived?"

The old man pointed toward the southwest, across the water. "This man sounds very powerful," said Charon. "And you're too young a fish, too small. You and I are jokes to the gods. Go away."

"I can't," Indy said. He stood his ground. Okay, he thought. Orpheus had to charm Charon to take him across the river Styx. Indy had better come up with something fancy here, too. "It's better if I'm so small," Indy said. "A big fish would frighten him. But he won't be afraid of me even when I get close."

The old man considered this and finally nodded. "That is your fate," he said. "But not mine."

"Yesterday I didn't know who you were. Someone led me here because you're the only person who can take me to find the man with the cane. It's a matter of life or death, Charon."

"How am I supposed to take you?"

"In your boat. You have one, don't you?"

The man looked surprised. "How do you know I have a boat?"

How did I know? Indy thought. His name is Charon and he lives by water. How could he *not* have a boat?

"I took a good guess," Indy said with a smile. "Let's go!"

Chapter 10

"Hold on tight!" Charon shouted.

The small sailboat rose and dipped wildly with the waves. The water seemed to be toying with the tiny vessel, slapping it this way and that just to prove who was mightier.

But Indy knew there was no turning back. Every time the stinging salt spray made him close his eyes, he saw Elyse being kidnapped in the carriage. No matter how mighty the sea was, Indy had to be stronger. Or at least more determined.

He sat in the middle of the twenty-foot wooden skiff, his arms grasping the mast. The only thing louder than the snapping of the tall sail above him was Charon, the canemaker. He was standing at the helm, bellowing an endless song in Greek in his off-key voice.

Forget the sea, Indy thought. The real question was: Could he stand the whole two-hour trip to the island of Aegina with that man singing? After just one hour, Indy was thinking about swimming for it.

"What are you singing?" Indy called to the old man.

"I sing my song to the gods," Charon shouted. "My song says, 'Oh, Poseidon, god of the sea, do not swallow my little boat. If it pleases you, let me pass over your great waters. Oh, Zeus, god of gods, have mercy on my little boat. I am but a poor messenger of troubled souls. Let me finish my journey from life to death.'"

"Cheerful," said Indy.

When Charon started singing again, Indy wondered if the gods were holding their ears. "I thought *I* was Orpheus," he grumbled. "*I'm* supposed to do the singing."

A while later, the waters calmed to an almost dead stillness and Charon guided the boat in to the small island of Aegina.

It seemed to take forever for the boat to drift into the bay marina. While he waited to go ashore, Indy stared at the white beaches, green forested hills, and houses of stucco and stone. The island was surprisingly pleasant. It didn't look like the underworld to Indy—except for the fact that Markos Kourou lived there.

Charon tied the boat to the long wooden dock, then clamped a strong, bony hand on Indy's shoulder and turned him toward the little village. "This is Ayía Marína," said Charon. He pointed with his other hand. "And that is the street where you'll find the house of the man who bought the Medusa-head cane."

Indy's eyes followed Charon's finger and saw a street leading uphill. "Which house is it?" he asked.

Charon held up three gnarled fingers. "I remember only three things about the place," he said. "The house was stucco. There was a walled garden. And in the front yard there was an olive tree. That's what I remember."

"Stucco, walled garden, olive tree—okay. Wait for me here," said Indy. He started to march off, then stopped. "There's going to be someone with me when I come back," Indy said. "And we'll be in a big hurry to leave."

"I will wait until I know you cannot return," said Charon.

Indy wasn't sure what that meant, but he didn't like the sound of it. "Don't worry. I'll be back," he said, hurrying toward Kourou's street.

Aegina was much smaller and quieter than Athens. That's probably why it was a perfect hideout for Markos Kourou, Indy thought. There weren't many people around.

Indy passed a wooden boat that was resting overturned on the wharf. Five fishermen in thick white wool sweaters and short-brimmed, squat black caps were sitting on it. They were sewing and repairing their fishing nets. They fell into silent stares as Indy walked by.

Did *they* know Kourou? Indy wondered. Did *they* work for him? He didn't dare ask.

Tap-tap. Tap-tap.

The sound made Indy turn instantly, looking for a cane.

But it was only an old woman tapping her clay pipe on the stone steps of her house. Lying at her feet were parts of some fish she had just cut up.

The street Charon had pointed to was on

a gently sloping hill. Houses of different sizes and styles were built close together, with only a small space between them.

Indy ran up the street, scanning each house as he went. They were *all* stucco—big deal. Everything in Greece was stucco! That wasn't a problem. The problem was that one house had an olive tree but no wall. The next had a wall but no garden. A third had a large garden on all sides, with fruit trees and many olive trees. Not exactly what Charon had said. None of the houses matched the description Charon had given him.

Indy was about to walk back to the bottom of the street and start again, when suddenly he heard the sound of heavy breathing—and had the feeling he was being watched. He turned, facing the last house on the dead-end street—the one at the very top of the hill. The house seemed to have an enormous yard in the rear, which sloped back down to the water. But the front of the house was surrounded by a tall stucco wall that enclosed a small garden. The only thing missing was the olive tree.

Indy looked through the iron bars of the front gate. Something *was* watching him! As soon as their eyes met, the enormous dog began to snarl and growl.

Indy jumped back fast, then stared at the animal. It was the largest Irish wolfhound he'd ever seen—almost the size of a small horse. The animal tried to force its huge head between the bars of the gate. It dug at the ground, trying to reach Indy.

I've got to get out of here, Indy thought, backing away.

But suddenly a picture flashed into his mind. It was a picture of Cerberus, the huge, mythological dog that guarded the gates of the underworld.

Indy took a step closer and looked at the house again. It wasn't quite the house Charon had described. But who cares? Indy thought. Olive trees die. This house had a huge dog guarding it—just like Cerberus guarded the underworld! It had to be Kourou's house—and Elyse had to be inside!

But there was only one way to know for sure.

"Good dog," Indy said, moving closer. "Good boy."

As soon as Indy moved, the dog went crazy. It whipped around in circles, throwing its body against the iron gate, frantically trying to get through.

Okay, Indy thought, if I'm Orpheus, then maybe I can charm Cerberus with my song.

Grabbing the gate and pulling it toward him slowly, Indy edged into the garden. At the same time, he began to sing the first song that came into his head.

"Oh, Poseidon, god of the sea, do not swallow my little boat. If it pleases you, let me pass over your great waters. Oh, Zeus—"

Until that moment, the dog had been growling, but not loudly enough to be heard inside the house. Now it let out a deafening howl.

Then the animal leaped.

With its teeth bared and saliva dripping from its mouth, it lunged straight at Indy's throat!

Chapter 11

Indy crashed into the iron gate, pushed backward by the weight of the leaping, snarling dog. The gate swung wide open and Indy almost fell. But the dog kept moving past him—into the street—carried by its own momentum.

In one single quick move, Indy pulled the gate closed again and latched it. The dog jumped on the gate, barking wildly. But now it was outside, trying to get *in*!

Indy didn't wait. He turned and ran like mad. The dog's barks grew fainter as he rounded the corner to the back of the house.

From the backyard, he glanced out past the grassy hill that fell steeply to the beach. A large boat was coming in from the sea, arriving at a private dock just behind the house.

Visitors?

Quickly Indy turned around to scout his next target—the back door. One second he was hiding among some sheets that hung from clotheslines and flapped in the breeze. The next minute he was at the back door, opening it and slipping inside.

Kitchen, Indy said to himself, scanning the room. He took it all in: a small table, a cabinet with china, shelves with pans, a large wood-burning stove.

He crept to the door by the oven, but backed away quickly. There were voices, two men's voices, speaking Greek—and coming closer! Had they heard the dog? Were they looking for Indy?

Heart pounding, Indy hurried to a different door and opened it a crack. It led to a long, dark hallway with more doors. Big house, Indy thought as he darted down the hall and ducked into the first room on the left.

Maybe Elyse will be in here, Indy hoped.

But the instant he entered the room, he froze. In the middle, caught in the light through a lace-curtained window, sat an old woman in a rocking chair. Her eyes were closed and her mouth had fallen open. She was snoring softly, her arms hanging limply over the arms of the chair.

Hope you're a heavy sleeper, Grandmother, Indy said to himself, backing out of the room. He hurried to the end of the hallway, where he found a stairway leading up. As he began to creep up the stairs, he heard a man's voice behind him, talking to the old woman down the hall.

Was it Kourou? Indy still didn't know if he was in the right house!

He took the steps two at a time, until he reached the second-floor landing.

Now what? More doors. This was like playing Russian roulette. Kourou could be waiting in any chamber! And so could Elyse.

After listening for sounds from inside, Indy slipped into the nearest room and closed the door quickly. Then he turned to see where he was—and how long he would be safe.

"Ahhhgh!" Indy gasped, then clamped his hand over his mouth to muffle the noise.

This is it! he thought. It's Kourou's house, all right. And I've just walked into his treasure room!

Everywhere he looked—on shelves, on pedestals, on tables, on the walls—were pieces of ancient art. Pottery, jewelry, paintings, sculpture. It was a breathtaking collection of works from almost every civilization. But the greatest number of pieces were from ancient Greece.

Indy scanned the room from one end to the other, looking for the one piece of antiquity he wanted to see most—the golden Pietroasa bowl.

It's not here, he said to himself finally. What did you do with it, Kourou? And what did you do with Elyse?

Rushing footsteps in the hall, coming his way. Quick—hide! Indy told himself. But where?

There was a connecting door that led into the next room. Indy slipped through the door and made his escape just as the footsteps stopped outside the treasure room.

Now where am I? he wondered.

Bookcases, a large desk piled with stacks of papers, notebooks, newspapers. It was an office. I'm getting closer to the black heart of Markos Kourou, Indy thought.

He looked quickly through the papers on

the desk. There were newspaper clippings lying on top. Some had articles about various pieces of Greek art that had recently been discovered.

The rat must be making out his wish list, Indy said to himself.

Then suddenly Indy's eyes fell on a small black book with a dozen pages. He picked it up and opened it.

Eureka! It was Markos Kourou's passport! Indy read the name, then flipped the pages and found the proof. Kourou had been in Rumania when the Pietroasa bowl was stolen!

Indy put the passport in his pocket. Kourou won't be doing any traveling for a while—not if I have anything to say about it, Indy thought, and smiled.

Hey—it's too quiet, Indy suddenly realized. He listened again. No footsteps. Time to get out while the going's good.

Stepping softly, Indy moved back to the connecting door—the one that led into the treasure room. He put his ear to the door and listened. Nothing.

Okay—great, he thought. He turned the knob and opened it.

Yikes!

Filling the doorway like a huge stone statue was the same Greek guy who had chased him through the streets of Athens.

Indy didn't have to think twice. He spun around and made a fast dash for another door, one leading into the hall. He tore it open—and bumped into another statue. A strong hand immediately pushed him back.

"Impossible!" Indy exclaimed. The same man was at *this* door, too! As if by magic, he had Indy trapped between two doors at once!

"Wait a minute. What's going on?" Indy said. "Twins?"

"Shut up," said the one who was closest to Indy—right before he swung his fist.

Indy felt the punch hit his jaw and slumped to the floor, unconscious.

Someone's humming, Indy thought. No, someone's moaning. Slowly it dawned on him. *He* was the one moaning! He was waking up. His jaw hurt. Then he noticed that his arms and legs hurt too.

"Where am I?" he said. He opened his eyes and answered his own question. He was in a comfortable living room, sitting in a soft chair. Sunlight poured in the windows. Vases of dried flowers sat on tables. It would have been cozy—except for the fact that his arms and legs were tied with a heavy rope. He couldn't move.

"Hey!" Indy shouted.

The old woman tottered into the room. She didn't seem to know or care that Indy was there.

"Do you speak English? *Omilíte angliká?*" Indy asked.

Without a word she walked over, slapped his face, and left the room.

"I thought water and jam was a nicer tradition," Indy called after her.

A moment later, one of the curly-haired twins came into the room and smiled, seeing that Indy was awake.

"Where's your boss?" Indy said, struggling against the ropes. "Where's Kourou?"

"Shut up," said the man. He said the two words slowly, as if he were practicing them.

"Who taught you manners? The old woman?" Indy asked.

"Shut up," he said again.

Behind him, the other twin came in eating an orange, peel and all. Indy looked at the two of them side by side. Twin Gods of the Sore Jaw. They both wore the same traditional loose tunic of coarse cloth. The only difference Indy could see was that the one who had hit him wore a red sash around his long shirt. The other one, eating the orange, had no belt but wore a gold cross around his neck.

"How about untying these ropes?" Indy said to the brother with the orange and the gold cross.

The man looked at Indy blankly and said, "Shut up."

"Is that all you two can say?" asked Indy.

"As a matter of fact, it is," said a curt voice off to the side.

Indy's eyes followed the voice to the doorway. A man stood there. Indy hadn't noticed him come in. He was short and slightly plump, dressed in a black suit and a dark hat. In his black-gloved hand was an ebony cane, the gold handle of which he tapped against his cheek. His long hair was black, the same as his bushy mustache.

Kourou at last, Indy thought. But he looked nothing like the man Kalitsa had described!

"That's all the English I've taught them," said the man. He spoke with a British accent. "You've been looking for Markos Kourou. Here I am."

Indy tried to sink lower in the chair as Kourou came near. But he couldn't help staring at Kourou's face. Close up, his hair and mustache looked odd. Indy realized that they were both fake. And there was something else—something strangely familiar about him.

Then, when Kourou was only three feet away, Indy looked deep into the man's watery blue eyes—and suddenly he knew.

"No, it can't be," Indy said, his voice trembling. "You're not Markos Kourou. I know who you are. You're Professor Wolcott!"

Chapter 12

"Professor Wolcott?" the man in black said. "Everyone knows he's a harmless old windbag—more interested in talking about rare and ancient treasures than owning them."

Kourou's laughter was light and mocking. He kept it up as he reached with a gloved hand to peel off his black hairpiece and black mustache. Then the laughter stopped.

Don't say anything, don't show surprise, Indy tried to tell himself. But he couldn't help letting out a gasp. It *was* Nigel Wolcott! His father's old professor! That useless old man was really Markos Kourou! Except now he looked different—as if all the kindness had been squeezed out of his face.

"How can a boy have found out what

men all over the world could not? Tell me that," Nigel said, highly annoyed. He started pacing the floor a few feet from Indy. He glanced over at the twin brothers, who were sitting by the door like watchdogs. Then he stopped in front of his captive. "I *have* surprised you, haven't I? I can see it on your face."

"I just can't believe a scholar could do something so low," Indy said.

"Oh, but that's what made it so easy, dear boy," Nigel said. "As an expert on ancient artifacts, I could come and go anywhere and no one suspected a thing. Museums and private collectors all over the globe *begged* me to examine their antiquities. Of course, I was only too happy to oblige, taking note of which were the finest."

"So you could go back and steal them," Indy said.

"Well, I couldn't steal them myself, of course," Nigel said. "Much too risky. I would surely have been recognized. But as Markos Kourou—and with the help of my assistants, Jannis and Theo—I could actually be right there and experience the thrill when the pieces were stolen."

"And if anyone saw you—all they saw was a Greek man with a fancy Medusa-head cane," Indy said.

"Correct," Nigel said. "It was a splendid disguise, if I do say so myself. I think I've always had a bit of the actor in me. Perhaps I should have gone on the stage."

Indy shook his head. The man sounded like he thought the whole thing had just been a big game!

"With a Greek name and a fake mustache, I guess you fit right in on the island of Aegina," Indy said.

"You do figure things out quickly, lad. Such a bright and agile mind. I envy you your youth," said Nigel. "If I had started stealing when I was your age, just think of the treasures I'd own."

"I've seen your collection," Indy snapped. "You don't own any of them. They belong to museums."

"Indiana, you've lived with your father too long," Nigel said. "You're beginning to sound as tiresome as he does."

"Leave my father out of this. He trusted you," Indy said angrily.

"Your father is a fool," Nigel said. He said

it as calmly as if he were ordering something to eat. "For example, after you left this morning, I told him that I was going to the library and I expected to be gone all day. A preposterous lie, but he completely believed me."

"He's an old-fashioned guy," Indy said. "He believes what people tell him."

Nigel nodded and smiled smugly. "It astounds me that *he* could raise a son as clever as you. I always wanted a son."

"You mean you wanted an accomplice," Indy said. "You wouldn't know what to do with a son."

Nigel's face changed and he took a slow, deep breath. Indy stiffened. Something was about to happen. Indy gave a tug on the ropes around his arms and legs. They were as tight as ever.

"Well, I can see that I've got to decide what to do with you—and the policeman's daughter," Nigel said, sounding angry.

"Where is Elyse?" Indy demanded. "Is she here?"

"She is being taken care of," said Nigel.

Indy suddenly yelled as loudly as he could. "Elyse!"

"She can't answer you, I'm afraid," said Nigel. "We had to put a gag in her mouth. She has an annoying habit of screaming at the most inappropriate times, and we were afraid the neighbors would hear her."

"What's all this noise?" said a woman as she came into the room. Indy looked up to see who it was, and his mouth fell open. Kalitsa! She walked up to Nigel and kissed him on the cheek. "I heard someone yelling. Is everything all right, dear?"

"Nothing I can't handle, lamb," said Nigel, looking at Indy.

Kalitsa smiled at Indy as she picked up the orange cat that was following at her feet. Indy noticed the wedding ring on her finger—a gold ring. Then he remembered what Nigel had said. That she was the wife of a very good friend. A good friend, my foot. Indy felt sick. Why hadn't he guessed it?

"So he *was* there in the shop that day," Indy said to Kalitsa.

"Who was?" she asked.

"Nigel—Kourou—your husband—what's-his-name," said Indy with a jerk of his head toward Nigel.

"Oh, call me whatever you like," Nigel said.

"Don't tempt me," said Indy.

"No, he wasn't there that day. Why do you ask?"

"I saw his cane there," Indy explained.

"He always leaves his cane in the shop," Kalitsa said, stroking the cat under its chin. "You know, it really was quite good fortune that you and Naxakis's daughter came to the shop."

"I detest that man," Nigel said, interrupting. "He's been hounding us for years."

"That's why I decided to have Jannis and Theo get rid of his daughter for you, darling," Kalitsa said. "I knew that nothing in the world would cause Naxakis more pain than losing her."

"You and Nigel deserve each other," Indy said.

Abruptly she dropped the animal and moved closer to Indy. She removed his hat and stroked his head—the same way she had petted her cat, but without affection. "Does he have to be tied up, dear?"

"No," said Nigel. "I think it's time to untie him."

The way Nigel said "it's time" sent a chill down Indy's back.

As soon as Kalitsa loosened the ropes, Indy tried to make a dash for the door. But the minute he stood up, Theo and Jannis stood up too. It was no use. There were four of them in the room—plus the old woman was somewhere near. Who was that old woman, anyway? Probably the twins' grandmother, considering her attitude. And Elyse. Where was Elyse?

Indy sat down again, slumping.

"Come, come, Indiana. Be a good student and focus your attention on why you came here," Nigel said. "Aren't you going to ask me about the Pietroasa bowl?"

"I know it's not in your treasure room," Indy said. "I looked."

"Quite true," said Nigel. "And I'm not going to tell you where it is. But you could have had it. In fact, you had your hands on it once. Now you'll never see it again."

Had my hands on it? Indy hated Nigel's smile. Sly and proud.

"I haven't touched any bowls," Indy muttered.

"That will give you something to think

107

about. Now we must get on with things,"
said Nigel. "Jannis!" he called. The twin
with the gold cross around his neck came
alert. Then Nigel said something in Greek
that Indy didn't understand.

Suddenly Jannis and Theo came over and
yanked Indy to his feet.

"Wait! I'll make a deal with you!" Indy
gasped. That got Nigel's attention. Nigel sig-
naled the twins to let him sit down again.

"I seriously doubt if you have anything to
offer me," Nigel said.

"The old canemaker—Charon," said Indy,
thinking quickly. "I told him to wait for me
at the dock. I also told him to bring the
police if I wasn't back in an hour."

Nigel stepped back. He tapped his cane
on the floor while he examined Indy's face.

"Is he lying?" Kalitsa asked.

"We know he's a clever lad, but how
clever?" Nigel said. "Clever enough to make
a plan with the old canemaker? Or only
bold enough to lie?" He smiled and rapped
the cane handle in his hand. "Interesting
problem. What deal would you like to
make?"

Indy kept staring at Nigel, looking him

straight in the eyes. "Let Elyse leave with me, and I promise I won't go to the police until you've had time to get away."

"Ha ha," said Nigel dully. "You want the girl, not the bowl, not any of the treasures you saw in my room?"

Indy said nothing. He just glanced at the clock, as if to say: Hurry up and decide. The police will be here soon.

"Oh, I understand now," Nigel said. "Bless me, how could I have forgotten. You're Orpheus *Junior*—that's what your father called you." He gave Kalitsa an amused look. "The boy has the absurd idea that he is reliving the Orpheus legend. He's Orpheus, and that dreadfully stubborn girl is Eurydice. I guess that makes me Pluto, god of the underworld. And he wants me to free her!"

"What are you going to do, Nigel?" Kalitsa asked.

Nigel thought for a moment, stroking his round face with his gloved hand. "Perhaps I should make this legend come true," he said to Indy. "But this is *my* deal. Go back to your boat, Orpheus Junior. Leave the underworld, and I'll send Elyse along behind you.

You may listen for her footsteps. But no matter what you do, don't look back when you leave." He let a little chuckle escape when he said that. "Because if you turn around to look at her—I assure you, she will *die*."

"I want to see her first," Indy said. "I don't even know if she's here."

Instead of answering, Nigel simply shook his head.

"Okay, okay," Indy said, nodding to accept the deal.

Quickly Indy jumped up and went to the front door. Nigel and Kalitsa followed.

"You *will* give my warmest regards to your dear father, won't you?" Nigel said insincerely as he pushed Indy out the door.

It was hard to walk and not run away from the house. But Indy took it slowly, listening for Elyse's footsteps. When he was about ten paces away from the door, he heard a voice.

"Indiana!" called Nigel.

Indy froze. What did Nigel want? He started to turn around to see. But he stopped instead and called, "What?"

"Just testing," answered Nigel with a laugh. "Continue."

Slowly Indy moved toward the gate and opened it. He gave the dog waiting outside a look as he passed. It growled and barked as it ran back into the yard. Why don't I hear any footsteps? Indy wondered. Where is Elyse? Is Nigel really going to let her go? Or is this only a trick?

"No matter what you do, don't look back when you leave." Nigel's words echoed in Indy's head.

I *am* Orpheus, Indy thought again. But I refuse to make Orpheus's mistake.

Still, the silence was killing him. Why couldn't he hear—

There!

Footsteps, crunching the dirt, matching his own step for step!

She was there! Everything was all right.

Indy let out a breath of relief and walked faster. This was going to work out.

He was on the street now, going down the hill to the docks. And Elyse was still behind him. Orpheus and Eurydice—walking out of the underworld! Only this time, they were *both* going to make it. Two more minutes and they'd reach Charon's boat.

But something didn't seem right. What was it?

Her footsteps. They sounded funny.

Heavy. Not like the delicate young woman he had spent a whole day with.

A knot twisted in Indy's stomach. It's not her, he suddenly realized. It's someone else! One of the twins! His mind started racing.

Don't turn around, Indy told himself. Don't make the same mistake Orpheus made.

Indy's heart was racing as he slowed his own steps to a crawl. I am Orpheus, Indy thought. I must not make Orpheus's mistake!

But he was desperate to know who was behind him.

The footsteps moved closer. He could almost feel the person's breath on his neck.

Quickly Indiana Jones turned around and looked back.

Chapter 13

"Elyse!" Indy shouted as he turned to see who was behind him. But he called her name too soon. Because it wasn't Elyse. It was Jannis! Indy had been tricked!

Then Indy saw that Jannis was nervously clenching the Medusa-head cane.

Why does he have the cane? Indy wondered.

"Shut up," Jannis barked. "Shut up!" One hand gripped the shaft of the cane and the other yanked on the gold Medusa handle. A long steel blade slid out.

For a moment, Indy was held hypnotized by the blade. It flashed even brighter in the sun than the gold cross around Jannis's neck. Faster than Indy could see, Jannis swung his arm and the blade came right for Indy's heart.

Indy shouted and jumped back. This isn't funny, he thought. He's really trying to kill me!

Jannis raised his hand again, but this time Indy made a move to run to the right. Jannis moved in the same direction. Quickly Indy ducked and then dodged to the left. Jannis tried to turn, and his feet slipped on some loose gravel in the street. Down he went.

That was all the head start Indy needed. He began to run, but not for the dock and Charon's boat, not for safety. Instead, he ran back to Nigel's house because that's where Elyse was.

Panting, Indy ran through the gate and into the front yard, looking for a stick along the way to deal with the dog if he had to. But the animal was nowhere in sight. Strange, Indy thought. But lucky. Now he had a clear shot all the way to the front door. Hurry, Indy told himself. Jannis will be here any minute.

Indy's fists pounded on the door. "Elyse!" he called.

Inside the house the dog barked viciously,

jumping and scratching on the door with all its strength.

Indy backed off. What was the dog doing in the house all of a sudden? His brain raced. People keep guard dogs outside when they're home, to warn them. But they keep them *inside*, to guard the house, when they're gone! Indy thought.

Gone. That meant Nigel was escaping. And there was only one way he could do that—by sea.

"Elyse!" Indy shouted, so loud his lungs almost burst.

"Indiana!" a distant voice answered.

It was her! Her voice sounded like it had come from down the hill at the end of the backyard.

Indy ran around to the back. From the top of the steep hill he saw Nigel, Kalitsa, and the other twin, Theo. They were dragging Elyse with them as they hurried toward the large sailboat tied to the private wooden dock—the same boat Indy had seen arrive earlier.

Indy started down the hill. His legs pumped as hard as they could, half-running, half-slipping down the long slope. But Jannis was right behind him. Indy could hear the big man grunting as his feet thumped the soft dry grass.

As Indy hit the dock, the boat started to move away, gliding out to sea. But Indy took a chance. He leaped through the air—and landed on the deck of the boat.

Ooomph! Jannis landed an instant later—right on top of Indy!

Jannis's weight on Indy's chest forced the air out of his lungs. Before he could catch his breath, four hands began pulling him, dragging him across the deck.

There was no point in struggling. Indy already knew the strength and power of the twins. He let the two men stand him up facing Nigel, who sat with Kalitsa at the helm of the boat. Kalitsa appeared cool and calm, but Nigel looked flustered by Indy's unexpected arrival.

"You're the most uncooperative young man I've ever encountered," Nigel said, trying to sound in control. But Indy heard a note of frustration in his voice.

"You're not going to get away with this," said Indy.

"No? I'm shocked, truly shocked," Nigel said. "What a frightfully unoriginal thing for you to say. I expected better of you, Junior."

Indy opened his mouth to reply, but Nigel quickly waved his hand, signaling the twins to take Indy away. They dragged him to a storage hold at the rear of the boat, opened the hatch, and gave him a shove. He tumbled down four steep, narrow stairs, hurting his arms, his legs, and his back. When he landed, he tried to stand up and bumped his head on the low ceiling. The storage hold was no bigger than a cage.

"Indiana," said a familiar voice in the dark.

"Elyse," Indy said, relieved. "You're all right."

"I was so worried," Elyse said. She scooted over close to him.

"Don't worry. You're going to be okay," Indy said reassuringly.

"I was so worried about *you*," Elyse corrected him. "I was tied up in a room very close to you and I heard everything that was said. But they had a cloth around my mouth so I couldn't warn you. I'm glad you are all right."

"All right for now," Indy said.

"He's still going to kill us, isn't he?" Elyse asked.

I bet he's not planning to adopt us, Indy thought. But all he said was, "I don't know."

In the silence that followed, Indy tried to figure out what to do. He had come so close to what he wanted. He had uncovered Markos Kourou and found many stolen treasures. With a little more time and luck, he'd have had the bowl, too. Time and luck—how much did he have left? He'd have to make his own.

"Elyse, I've got a plan," Indy said. "If we can get out of here, I think we should jump—and try to swim for it."

"No, Indiana," said Elyse.

Her short answer caught him by surprise.

"What's the matter?" he asked. "Can't you swim?"

"No, not very well," she admitted. "But it does not matter how well you or I can swim. It's impossible. The waters are cold, too cold for swimming. The winter sea swallows up foolish people who try."

"Yes, but think about it. Do you want to take your chances with Nigel or the water?"

Instead of answering she leaned back against the steps and sighed. The boat pitched and rocked. Indy couldn't tell how much time went by, but enough for their small hold to get stuffy and hot.

Finally the hatch door above slid open, letting in a burst of light. Kalitsa leaned in, holding back her full dark hair. "Come up, please, both of you," she called, smiling and friendly. "Nigel has decided."

Elyse put her hand on Indy's arm, stopping him from getting to his feet. "Do you know what my father would do?" she asked. "My father wouldn't go. He always says life is mean-hearted enough, so what is the sense in cooperating?"

Indy smiled, but he moved toward the steps. "I like your father a lot," he said. "But if it looks like I'm not cooperating, Nigel's going to do something I'll hate."

She opened her deep, dark eyes wide. "What is that?"

"Hurt you," Indy said. He leaned over and whispered in her ear, "I'll go in the water first. Then you jump. We'll swim together."

"We'll die together," she whispered back.

On deck, the sunlight blinded him at first,

but after a moment Indy could see the twins, Theo and Jannis, at the helm. Kalitsa had moved to the back of the boat, away from everyone. Nigel was eating black olives and spitting pits into the water.

Indy looked off to the island behind them. Aegina looked small and far away—and so did Piraeus in the other direction.

"You can't escape, you know," Nigel said. "We're out too far for you to swim."

"It never crossed my mind," Indy lied. "Besides, I couldn't leave before you gave me a grade—could I, Professor Wolcott?"

Nigel looked at Indy and Elyse, considering this idea with a small smile. "Well, you certainly are a bright and eager young student," he said. "But I'm afraid I'm going to give you a failing mark for this course. Why didn't you learn your lesson from Orpheus and not look back? You know that I simply cannot let you live."

Before Indy could answer, Elyse charged forward and spit twice in Nigel's face.

"That is for my father and that is for me!" she shouted. "Now I have done everything I wanted to do in life. It doesn't matter what you do to me."

Nigel wiped his face with a linen hand-kerchief. "My dear girl, I must admit I won't be sorry to see you go. Jannis has requested to handle your death personally. I think he wants to make it up to me for bungling the job with your father."

Indy felt the electric shock of the words pass through Elyse and into him.

"But first," said Nigel, "I shall have to deal with Indiana."

"Uh, there's no hurry," Indy said.

"See if you don't think this clever," Nigel said. "Theo and Jannis will wrap you in fishing nets and throw you overboard. You'll struggle in the netting, of course, trying to break free. But you'll just tangle yourself all the more. Eventually, but not too quickly, you'll drown."

Indy looked at the water and instantly the words of the old woman came back to him. *Descend...down...into the depths of danger...and death!*

"Or if you'd prefer, I might ask Theo to knock you out first, so you won't suffer quite so much," Nigel said. "It's the least I can do for the son of an Oxford man. Old school tie and all that." Nigel motioned for the twins to come forward. "Let's have a go at it, shall we?"

"No thanks," Indy said, quickly darting toward the side of the boat. But Nigel stuck out his cane and tripped him. He went down hard on the deck, and before he could get up, Theo grabbed Indy's legs in a powerful grip. Jannis grabbed him around the chest and stood him up.

Indy kicked and twisted, fighting hard, but the twins were too strong. Jannis's iron arms clamped Indy from behind, crushing his chest. Theo kept a lock on his legs.

"Stop it! Stop it, you lunatics!" Elyse cried.

No one had been watching her, so they were all surprised when she gave Nigel a hard push. And then, without a look back, she ran to the side of the boat and jumped into the icy sea!

Chapter 14

Indy watched Elyse jump and heard her scream follow her into the water. But he couldn't make a move to join her—not with the twins holding him.

A moment after she hit the water, though, Theo let go. He turned his head to watch, to see if she would drown. That's when Indy did it. Bracing himself against Jannis, Indy yanked up his knees and then kicked out as hard as he could. His feet caught Theo right in the chest and sent him reeling backward.

"Bullseye!" Indy shouted.

When Indy's feet came down, he stomped them as hard as he could on the tops of Jannis's feet. Jannis yeowed in pain and for an instant his arms went slack—enough time for Indy to wriggle free. He pushed Jannis aside and threw himself into the icy water so fast that his hat went flying off his head.

The water was a shock, colder than he ever expected. Shaking and shivering, he could hardly move. Forget swim.

"Indiana!" Elyse called to him when he surfaced. The waves had already carried her fifty yards off.

Gotta get to her, he thought. But his body just wanted to coil up in a tight little ball to keep warm. He forced himself to take a stroke and then another. And another.

SPLASH!

What was that? Indy turned and saw Jannis coming after him, swimming like a racer. Doesn't he know the water's freezing? Indy wondered. Doesn't he ever give up?

Swim, breathe; swim, breathe. Indy tried to match his strokes to the chant, but his cold, wet clothes felt like weights, pulling him down.

Where was Jannis? He looked over his shoulder to check. No one was in sight. Jannis had been there a minute ago. Where was he now?

A wave suddenly washed over Indy, filling his mouth with salt water and seaweed.

Yuck! He tried to spit it out, but the sea-weed was forced in by the waves.

Maybe I can just stop swimming for a minute, Indy thought. Treading water, he reached up to pull the seaweed out of his mouth. That's when he felt something grabbing his legs—and pulling him down!

Salty water filled Indy's mouth and nose. Choking, he flailed his arms wildly, sinking fast. Through the bubbling water, he saw Jannis below him, smiling, pulling him farther down by the legs.

Indy kicked as hard as he could. Once. Nothing. Another kick. There! He hit Jannis in the nose! The Greek man's hands flew up to protect his face, and he let go.

I'm free, Indy thought, and he gave a powerful scissors kick toward the surface.

When he reached the top, he took in great gulps of cool air. But an instant later, Jannis popped up too. For a strange moment there seemed to be a truce between them. They stared at each other and coughed and breathed. It was almost as if Jannis had read Indy's thoughts—How can you be trying to kill me?—and couldn't think of an answer.

But with a new lunge, Jannis pushed Indy under the water again, taking him deeper than before.

And then suddenly everything became deathly still—and Jannis relaxed his grip. Indy saw him backing away, a look of horror on his face.

What's going on? Indy wondered. And then he saw it—a giant octopus, at least eight feet long. It was just a few feet below him!

In the next instant, the octopus reached up one long tentacle and wrapped it around Indy's waist.

No! Indy thought, watching the horrible creature below. He knew enough about octopuses to know that they didn't just grab their victims. They *bit* them and poisoned them with some kind of stuff that could paralyze a fish—or a kid.

Two lumpy black eyes twisted in the creature's ugly, formless face. Its eight knobby arms, thick as saplings, rippled like seaweed. Each tentacle was dark on top, with yellow-and-pink suckers below.

Indy tried not to struggle, but he was running out of air. All he could think about, all he wanted in the world, was to open his mouth and breathe.

Don't do it, he told himself. Hold your breath or you'll drown.

The octopus was pulling him down, wrapping another tentacle around his ankle. And something else was happening, too. Something strange. The skin of the octopus was changing to bright red.

He's angry, Indy thought. Or scared. He's going to bite me now.

And then all of a sudden, when Indy thought his lungs would burst, the octopus let go! Indy saw a flash of gold in the water from the cross on Jannis's neck—and the octopus moved toward it.

It must be attracted to the shiny gold, Indy thought as he pushed away.

The water churned bubbles and turned inky black. One after another the octopus wrapped its thick tentacles around Jannis. It pulled the man's torso to him as Jannis tore frantically at the monster's arms. Jannis's eyes were wide—and then he opened his mouth in a scream.

I can't help him, Indy thought. I can't hold my breath anymore. He kicked with all his might and broke for the surface.

Air! That's what he needed. Clean, fresh, beautiful air!

He floated for a moment, letting his lungs fill several times. Then he dove back down under the water. Was there anything he could do to save the drowning man?

But the waters were empty as far as Indy could see, except for a bit of black ink that remained. An awful sickness rose up from Indy's stomach. The monster was gone. And so was Jannis. Indy kicked for the surface again, thinking of the horror he had just escaped.

"Indiana!" Elyse paddled toward him from twenty feet away. On her head she had a brown, broad-brimmed hat. His hat!

"I was afraid that this hat was all I had to remember you by," she said as she came close. Her lips were blue, her teeth chattering, but still she managed a smile.

"Let's get out of here," Indy said. "Before Kourou comes back."

Indy looked over at Kourou's boat and almost smiled. One of the lines to the mainsail had come loose, and the sail was flapping freely in the wind. At least for a moment, the boat was stalled dead in the water.

"Follow me!" Indy shouted, starting to swim toward Piraeus.

Elyse tried to swim, but Indy could see that she was really just treading water. And not very well. He swam up beside her and started to put his arm around her back.

"Indiana, look over there!" Elyse said, nodding. "Another boat."

A small sailboat was riding the waves directly behind them. Its one large sail was filled tight with wind. It was traveling as fast as it could—and there was something familiar about it.

"Hey! I know that boat," Indy said, waving an arm as high above the water as he could. He started swimming again. "It's Charon. Hey! Over here!"

As the little boat came closer, Indy could see the bony, wrinkled canemaker at the helm. Charon stood and waved a cane in the air.

"Keep swimming!" Indy shouted to Elyse. "He sees us!"

Charon angled his little boat and came alongside Elyse. Reaching out with his cane, he helped her onto the boat first. Then he reached for Indy and pulled him in. He left them lying side by side on the wooden boat bottom, shivering and half-dead.

"I thought you didn't want to swim for it," Indy gasped. "You could have drowned."

"I tried to think, What would my father say?" she explained.

"What would he say?" asked Indy, barely able to talk above a whisper.

"He would say, 'Do exactly what Indiana Jones says. He would make a good policeman.'"

Charon came back with thick blankets. Briefly he explained how he knew to come rescue them—he'd seen Jannis following Indy down the street from Kourou's house.

"But the other boat?" Indy asked, lifting his head to the old man. "Where's Kourou now?"

"Sailing out to sea," Charon said as his strong, leathery hands tucked the blankets around them.

Indy slumped onto the boat's floor. He said I'd never see the Pietroasa bowl again, Indy thought. He must be taking the bowl with him!

130

Chapter 15

Shivering and weak, Indy propped himself up on shaky arms so he could see the water. He had to watch Nigel head out to sea and the Pietroasa bowl slip out of reach or it wouldn't be true. This wasn't how the journey was supposed to end. "Someday, Nigel," Indy muttered angrily.

Charon turned sunken blue eyes on him. "You must not think about the treasure you lost," he said. "Think about the treasure you have saved." He smiled warmly at Elyse before he moved back to the helm.

Elyse was safe. Cold and wet, but safe. She huddled close to Indy, wrapped in blankets. Wasn't she the real reason he had gone back to Nigel's house, raced onto his boat, and jumped into the freezing water?

Indy rested against the mast as the boat

headed back to Piraeus. But the bowl, he thought. And Nigel. He was going to knock me out so I'd drown faster—as a favor! I can't just forget a guy who wants to do a favor like that. Someday, Nigel.

It was nearly sunset when Indy helped tie Charon's boat to the dock near his shop. He and Elyse were in a hurry to see Ari, Indy's father, and the police. Indy held out his hand to thank Charon and say goodbye. But Charon wouldn't let it go.

"You must wait," Charon said, and he disappeared into his shack.

When he came out, he put a polished mahogany cane with a gold handle into Indy's hand.

"It's beautiful," said Indy. The golden handle had the image of a man in front and a woman standing behind him. "Who are they?"

"Orpheus and Eurydice," said Charon with a smile. "I made it many years ago and never wanted to sell it. Now I know why."

A few minutes later, Indy was tapping the cane anxiously on the floor of a donkey carriage, wishing they could go faster. But it still took an hour to get back to Athens.

The carriage stopped at Nigel's house first, because it was closer. Indy would see his father and then go with Elyse to see hers. After that, a police interrogation would seem like a breeze.

They ran into the house, through the entryway, and into the living room. There they found Indy's father sitting in a chair, writing in his notebook.

"Junior, is that you?" he asked, looking up.

His father seemed so surprised by their appearance that Indy looked at himself and Elyse in a gold-framed mirror on the wall. Their clothes were still wet and their faces were bruised.

"Are you all right?" asked Professor Jones. "Where have you been?"

"The underworld," said Indy. "Dad, this is Elyse, Ari Naxakis's daughter."

Professor Jones jumped to his feet and rushed to take her hands. "I'm so happy to see you, my dear."

"We're on our way to Ari's house, Dad, but I wanted you to know we're all right."

"But he's here!" said Professor Jones.

"Who? My father?" Elyse said. Her voice trembled.

Indy's father smiled. "He said he was too worried about you to be by himself. So he came in a carriage this afternoon. He's just down the hall in the study. I suggested that a good book would ease his mind."

Elyse ran from the room. A moment later Indy heard Ari's voice exclaiming in Greek.

"Nigel will be pleased to know that you're both safe," said Professor Jones.

"No, he won't," Indy said bitterly.

Professor Jones looked at him quizzically. "Well, you'll see for yourself, Junior," he said. "Nigel went to the library this morning. He'll be back any minute."

"He's not coming home, Dad," Indy snapped. "Ever."

His father raised an eyebrow. "You're acting most peculiarly, even for you, Junior," he said.

"Dad, you'd better sit down," Indy said. "I didn't just find Elyse. I found Kourou."

It took Indy a while to tell his father everything that had happened. When he got to the part about Kourou's identity, his father jumped to his feet and exclaimed,

"Nigel Wolcott is Markos Kourou? Preposterous!"

"Dad, I found his secret house. I saw all the stolen treasures," Indy said. "He and I stood as close as you and I are right now—and then he tried to kill me."

His father paced the room, shaking his head. "It's absurd," he said. "Do you hear me? Absurd! He's the most gentle and scholarly man I know."

"You knew him as one person, Dad," Indy said, "but I found out he was another. I know it's unbelievable, but you can see the treasures for yourself."

Still Professor Jones shook his head. Indy started pounding his fist on the back of a couch. "He's not coming home tonight—or any other night! He got away, Dad! He sailed off into the sunset, taking the Pietroasa bowl with him. And there was nothing I could do."

"The bowl," Professor Jones said, letting the word trail into a whisper. After a long silence, he started talking again. "Greed is a sly and powerful opponent," he said sadly.

"I know, Dad," Indy said. "I tried to stop him."

"If you did your best, son, then you're not to blame," Professor Jones finally said. He didn't smile, of course. But he didn't take his eyes away from Indy's either. He started to reach out and put a hand on Indy's shoulder. But he pulled it back when Ari wheeled himself into the room with Elyse.

"We must celebrate," Ari said, clapping the sides of his wheelchair. His face was wet with tears. So was Elyse's.

"Celebrate what, Ari?" said Indy. "Nigel got away."

"But my daughter is home! And Kourou is finished," said Ari. "Without Nigel Wolcott to make contacts for him, he is just a common thief. And I don't think he will be a very successful one, either. Mark my words, Indiana Jones: the bowl will reappear. You will hold it in your hands again someday."

"Someday." Indy repeated the word, picturing himself in the British Museum with the golden bowl in his hands. "Hold it in my hands?" he suddenly cried. "That's what Nigel said!"

"What did Kourou say?" Ari demanded quickly.

"He wanted to give me a hint, but l couldn't figure out what he meant before."

"But what did he say?" asked Ari.

"He said I'd had my hands on the bowl," Indy said, looking around the room. "But the only place he could have seen me touch a bowl was here in this house!"

"What?" said Professor Jones. "The bowl is here?"

"I didn't say it was still here," Indy said. "Maybe Nigel grabbed it before he left this morning. Who knows?"

"*I* know," said Professor Jones. "I saw him leave and he was empty-handed. I'm sure of it."

Indy's heart began to pound with excitement. He pushed back his hat and closed his eyes. He didn't want to see expectant faces staring at him while he thought. What bowl had he touched?

Suddenly he knew. He went straight to the dining room and stopped at the maple sideboard that stood along the wall.

"Is it here?" asked Elyse.

Indy picked up a bowl from the sideboard. Everyone looked excited at first, then crestfallen.

"That's not it, Junior," Professor Jones said irritably.

It was a dull blue-painted bowl with figs in it. But the moment Indy picked it up, he knew it felt like something he had held before. But not in Nigel's house. In the British Museum!

"Have a fig, Dad," Indy said.

"Junior, have you lost your mind altogether? This is no time for a snack," Professor Jones said.

"But I have to get rid of these figs somehow, Dad," Indy said, dumping them onto the sideboard. "So I can give you the Pietroasa bowl!"

It was true—and Indy's father knew it the minute he held the bowl. It had been painted with a thick coat of blue paint to hide the treasure underneath.

In the next hour, Indy watched his father remove the paint. Slowly gold began breaking through like sunlight through clouds. Soon all of the bowl's etched figures emerged under his father's careful hands.

"May I hold it, Dad?" Indy asked. When his father handed over the golden treasure, Indy stared at the sixteen figures etched in a circle around the inside of the bowl.

Orpheus was on the bowl several times—once with a raven on his shoulder! And there were other gods, too, some from the Orpheus story and some from other myths. A figure riding a horrible sea beast was supposed to be Pluto or his brother Poseidon, king of the sea. Pluto's young wife, Persephone, was on the bowl as well.

As Indy studied the bowl, he realized that it was sort of like looking at a diary of the last two days. So many figures on the bowl matched the people he had met in real life! He even saw the goddess of fortune—just like the old fortuneteller at the Parthenon—touching Orpheus with her wand. And there were pictures of the mythological twins, Castor and Pollux. They were like Jannis and Theo, Indy thought.

According to the legends, one of the twins was mortal and the other was a god. But which was which? Indy couldn't remember.

Maybe Jannis didn't die in the arms of the octopus after all, Indy thought.

"It's amazing," Indy said to his father. "So many things that happened to Orpheus on this bowl happened to me. The whole time

I've been in Athens, I've been reliving an ancient Greek legend."

"I can see that, Junior," Professor Jones said, clearing his throat. "I just can't explain it."

"The only difference is," Indy said, "I managed to *save* Eurydice! I saved Elyse."

"Ha! You saved no one," said Elyse.

"Huh?" Indy blinked.

"I am Ari Naxakis's daughter," she said, with her hands on her hips. "I do not get saved. I save myself!"

Indy was stunned. "You *what*?" he sputtered. Then he shook his head and looked at his father in exasperation.

"You see, Junior," Professor Jones said. "It's true what I've always told you."

"What does your father always say?" asked Elyse with intense curiosity.

Professor Jones gave Elyse a small smile. "I always tell him: They just don't make legends the way they used to!"

HISTORICAL NOTE

The Pietroasa bowl is a real object that was unearthed in 1837 in Rumania, along with twenty-one other precious artifacts. Scholars believe the golden bowl was probably made sometime during the third or fourth century A.D.

It is true, as Professor Wolcott told Indy's father, that a replica of the bowl *was* made in 1867 while the bowl was on loan to the British Museum. The real bowl was then returned to Rumania, where it was supposed to stay.

The bowl is called an Orphic bowl because Orpheus appears on it in several places. But the Orpheus legend—the story about his trip to the underworld to get Eurydice back—is not exactly shown on the bowl. Instead, there are various Greek gods, some of them from the Orpheus story and others who simply represent important aspects of a young man's journey toward wisdom and knowledge.

The sixteen figures on the bowl include Orpheus with a raven on his shoulder; Pluto and his wife, Persephone; Persephone's mother, Demeter; Tyche, the goddess of fortune; Agathodaemon, the god of good fortune; the twins, Castor and Pollux; and Apollo, the god of light and truth.

Pluto is also called Hades in Greek mythology. And sometimes the underworld itself is called Hades. It is a place where the dead go as soon as they die.

Although there is no record of the Pietroasa bowl ever having been stolen from Rumania in the winter of 1914, it did in fact disappear a few years later. During World War I it was taken to Moscow to protect it from the invading German soldiers. There, however, the Russian Communists melted it down for the gold after they came to power in 1917.

As a result the replica, which can still be seen in the British Museum, is the only evidence of the bowl that remains today.

TO FIND OUT MORE...

Usborne Illustrated Guide to Greek Myths and Legends by Cheryl Evans and Anne Millard. Published by Usborne Publishing Ltd. and EDC Publishing, 1985. This short introduction to Greek mythology and ancient Greece features great color pictures and famous Greek stories about Orpheus, Medusa, Perseus, and others. It also has information about Greek religion and history and a handy "Who's Who" guide to gods, heroes, and monsters. Maps, index.

Gods, Men & Monsters from the Greek Myths by Michael Gibson. Published by Peter Bedrick Books, 1991. Color and black-and-white drawings, index.
D'Aulaires' Book of Greek Myths by Ingri and Edgar d'Aulaire. Published by Dell Publishing, 1962. Color and black-and-white drawings, index.

Of the many longer books available on Greek mythology, these two collections are particularly good. Both offer full versions of all the major Greek myths—tales of loyalty, trickery, and revenge—and dramatic illustrations.

Ancient Greece (Eyewitness Books) by Anne Pearson. Published by Alfred A. Knopf, Inc., 1992. Go back in time and discover ancient Greece! Hundreds of full-color photographs and drawings with vivid captions present classical Greek art, architecture, battle armor, clothing, crafts, and more. Covers the country's amazing history from the Bronze Age to the rule of Alexander the Great. Maps, index.

Greece (Countries of the World) by Peggy Hollinger. Published by The Bookwright Press, 1990. Don't just take Indy's word for it—find out for yourself what the Parthenon and the streets of Athens really look like. Photos of ancient and new sites plus an interesting text give the flavor of city life in Greece. Also covered in this introduction to modern Greece are such subjects as transportation, education, sports, family life, food, religion, and festivals. Maps, glossary, index.

Tentacles: The Amazing World of Octopus, Squid, and Their Relatives by James Martin. Published by Crown Publishers, Inc., 1993. Exciting color photos and drawings of octopuses show just what Indy was up against in his almost fatal underwater encounter! The text gives all kinds of information about these fascinating creatures—their habits of feeding, defense, movement, reproduction, and more. Also covered are nautilus, squid, and cuttlefish. Glossary, index.

Music (Eyewitness Books) by Neil Ardley. Published by Alfred A. Knopf, Inc., 1989. Learn about the lyre, the instrument with which Orpheus charmed the powerful god of the underworld. In addition to lyres and harps, this introduction to sound and music has hundreds of color photographs and drawings of many other instruments. Index.